Myra

The Girl...the Woman...the Legend

Shirley Proctor Twiss

FpS

Greenville, S.C.

Myra: The Girl...the Woman...the Legend
by Shirley Proctor Twiss

Copyright © 2018 by Shirley Proctor Twiss

Requests for permission should be addressed to:

Fiction Addiction Publishing Services
1175 Woods Crossing Rd., #5
Greenville, S.C. 29607
864-675-0540
www.fiction-addiction.com

Cover photograph is the author's grandmother, Vida Sheppard McIntyre. Myra's story is a work of fiction, but the author was inspired by the faith, principles and love of her "Grandma Mac."

Cover and book design by Vally Sharpe

ISBN-13: 978-1-945338-92-2

Printed in the United States of America.

This book is dedicated to the gracious, gentle, kind and giving people of The Philippine Islands.

May they have peace in their homeland.

Author's Note

Writing a fourth book was never in my plans. Three times I firmly said, "This is my last." I should have learned to "Never say Never."

Again, I caution you that being a bona fide daughter of the South gives me the liberty of using dialogue that is uniquely accurate for the speech of my characters at that time period and in the location of rural Georgia. English teachers, put away your red pens—errors are intentional.

From Myra to Laura ended with the death of beloved character, Myra, and the emergence of granddaughter, Laura, to carry forth the legacy. I felt I had definite closure and no more stories. I was free to spend my time reading long novels of my favorite authors, watching recorded old movies, volunteering at places close to my heart, travel, long visits with family and friends, and whatever suited my fancy.

However pleasant my days (there is always a however in my decisions), something was lacking. I realized that void could only be filled by writing. I had abandoned characters who also had a story waiting to be shared.

The eight short stories will give you the background of characters from Book I-III who influenced Myra's life to give her happiness and sometime turmoil.

In the ending novella, her granddaughter Laura displays Myra's soul through her faith and dedication to "the least of these" when she accompanies her Episcopal priest husband, Paul, to an assignment on the Philippine island of Mindanao.

In writing the novella, I returned to memories of a special time in my life. The story enabled me to tie my faith and teaching experience into this remarkable setting with people I quickly learned to love and respect.

Salamat and Peace,
Shirley

Contents

The Short Stories

Sisters-in-Law 1

Father and Son 15

Schoolmarm 25

Sisters 36

Rosa 45

Mrs. Rosenberg 54

The Country Bride 69

Mr. Porter 83

Mindanao

Chapter I: 2000 99

Chapter II 111

Chapter III 117

Chapter IV 122

Chapter V 131

Chapter VI 147

Chapter VII 151

Chapter VIII: 2001-2005 160

Chapter IX: 2006 169

Chapter X: 2007 176

Epilogue 181

Acknowledgments 185

About the Author 187

The Short Stories

Sisters-in-Law

The close of another day found Olieta half-dozing in a rocker between her Mama and Papa. Sitting beside a crackling fire on this first cool evening of fall was especially cheerful. Supper was sitting contentedly in her stomach. The sighs of Papa told that he had enjoyed the cured ham, grits, stewed apples and hot biscuits she had prepared. Few words were said, and each family member seemed to be lost in their thoughts and hypnotized by the flames dancing around the aged oak logs.

Olieta was her name, but she was usually referred to by townsfolks as "Olieta MacTavish, the old maid." The term was not intended to be uncomplimentary or disrespectful to this highly regarded local lady. "Olieta MacTavish, the piano teacher" or "Olieta of the MacTavish family" would have been a more appropriate identification. Although she had only passed her fortieth birthday, Olieta was not disturbed to hear herself described as someone without hope for a husband. She was proud to be a MacTavish and honored to be an offspring of one of the most respected families in the town of Glencoe.

If she had looked for a beau, she could have found one. She had watched disdainfully as her sisters married hard scrabble farm boys or day wage earners who would never amount to a row of sticks. In only a few years her sisters turned from "one of the pretty MacTavish girls" into faded beauties who worked from dawn to dark, birthed too many babies and dealt with a husband who did as he pleased.

No Sir-ree, that was not the way I want to spend my life. That was her come back when asked if she had ever thought of marrying, and that satisfied their curiosity. No one suspected that once her heart had been stirred by someone she thought worthy of her love—but only once.

Old age had crept up fast after the death of her twin sister, Ovieta. Too soon, she started putting her hair into a bun like an old lady, wearing only dark clothes and seldom letting a smile reach her face. She had taken on most of the household chores and care of her younger siblings, especially James. Her ma kept having more babies and each one was handed to an older sister to tend. James had been given to her with the instruction, "James is yore baby. Take care of him." She took the role seriously, and from that moment on, she treated him as her special gift and did everything to please him. The death of Ovieta came shortly after the birth of James, and that made him even more precious to his older sister.

The town folks looked at her with concern, shook their heads and murmured "Pore thing will never get over the sorrow of losing her twin sister." This brought a silent snicker to Olieta, because she had welcomed trading her conniving sister for a sweet baby brother.

"Ain't it a mite soon to be makin' a fire, Sister?" asked her papa.

She felt a little hurt because she thought he was enjoying the warmth taking the chill off the air but would never show this in her reply. "Papa, the air changed from hot to cool so fast that I was afraid you and Mama would take a chill "

"It is a might chilly, but we could have done without a fire. We might need this wood later when it really turns cold." Papa always had the last word.

They were interrupted by the sound of horse hooves and rattle of a buggy arriving. "There's James," his mother said. "I was startin' to worry 'bout him. He shouldn't be drivin' that buggy in the dark."

Olieta always came to her brother's defense. In her eyes, he could do no wrong. "That mare knows the way home even in the dark. You know how James is when he gets out with his friends. Everybody loves to be with him, and he just hates to break away."

Papa's only comment to that was, "Huh." He knew the ways of young men in the MacTavish family. They liked to have a good time enjoying drinking and pretty women. James was reveling his manhood like all the MacTavish boys before him.

James walked into the room, but he was not alone. "Mama, Papa, Sister, this is Myra. We got married today." Holding his hand was a young girl with tawny skin, big dark eyes, long black hair and a frightened look.

Olieta looked back into the fire. Papa again commented, "Huh." Mama was the only one to speak. "Take her on back to yore room and have her put her things away. Rosa cleaned yore room good today and put on clean sheets."

The family continued to stare into the fire and hardly gave the young girl a glance. Myra knew she should say something to them, but since all she could see was the backs of their heads, she softly said, "Pleased to meet y'all." There was no reply.

James was eager to take his bride into his bedroom for their wedding night. He had been filled with desire for this young girl since he first saw her riding in a wagon down the main street of Glencoe. After getting to know her, he knew without a doubt that he was in love and thought of marriage for the first time in his life.

He did not want to leave Myra alone but knew he must say good night to his family and find a way to ease the shock this must have been for them.

After leading Myra to his room, he kissed and held her before saying, "I better go get this straight with Mama and Papa. You go on and get into bed, and I'll be back in a few minutes."

He was most fearful of Olieta's tongue, but he had to assert that Myra was now his wife; his sister could not continue to run his life. He stood in front of the fireplace and faced them.

"I know this is a shock to y'all, but I want you to welcome Myra into the family. I love her so much, and I know you will too if you will just give her a chance."

Olieta shook with rage as she said, "It will be a cold day in hell when that happens. Where did you drag that thing up from? She's some of the trash movin' in here from Washington County and trying to take over Glencoe. Most of 'ems half breeds. She shore looks like it with that long stringy black hair."

"Son, I don't know what brought this on so quickly, but yore papa can get you out of it." His mama was suspicious.

Olieta added, "You know she will never fit in with the family. Remember that the MacTavish family holds a place of respect in the county. You can't drag in someone like that and expect us to accept her."

James exploded at that. "Dammit to hell, I am tired of y'all trying to run my life. I married her because I love her more than anything. She is better than any of the MacTavish because she has a good heart. If she leaves, I leave with her." With that he stormed into the bedroom.

As he was leaving, Olieta added. "You better come back here. Once you go into that bedroom, there ain't nothin' Papa can do to help you get away from her."

James did not reply. His was headed to his beautiful bride.

"Papa, you've got to put a stop to this right now. Most likely she's already pregnant, and it ain't even his baby. James don't know nothin' about that kinda woman."

"Olieta, that's enough. I don't want you to say another word about this. James is a grown man and a smart man. He knows what he's doin'. She's just a young girl, and I believe she'll make him a good wife. Sides that, it's time we got some new blood in this family. Look how scrawny the young'uns are beginning to look." Papa had listened to what his son said about giving the girl a chance and also knew his son had better judgement than Olieta was crediting to him.

Mrs. MacTavish spoke for the first time. "Olieta, that kinda talk is what has kept you sittin' by our fire instead of having a husband and family of yore own. James ain't yore's to keep like when he was a baby."

Olieta was shocked that her mama and papa had taken the side of this half-breed. She got up so fast that her chair fell over with a bang and stormed out of the room.

The chilly bedroom made her regret leaving the fire, but she would not give them the pleasure of her listening to more about James' foolishness. Tomorrow would be too late to turn back what had happened.

It won't last. As soon as her belly pops out in a week or so, he'll know what he's married, and she will be gone as quick as she came.

As she climbed between the crisp cold sheets, her thoughts went back to James climbing into her bed and snuggling when he was a small boy. She would pull him as close as possible without smothering him. She respected her mama and papa, but James was her only love. Even as he got older, he would often come to her and sit on the side of her bed when he got home in the late evening. It was a pleasure to hear him tell her about his evening. Usually, he smelled of liquor and perfume---but she didn't object. He was a MacTavish, and all the men in the family had a little streak of wildness in them. He would grow out of it when he settled down with a good woman who was worthy to be a MacTavish.

Such thoughts would not allow sleep so she wrapped the quilt around her and went to the desk drawer. She had almost stopped opening this drawer, but tonight its contents filled her mind. Under a stack of saved letters was a small, tintype photograph of a young man with a full head of hair and a stern look. Folks never smiled when having a photograph taken. On the back was signed "To Ovieta, from your faithful admirer, Noah."

She had found this when she cleared out her twin sister's belongings after her death. *Why did he give the photograph to my sister? He was meant to be my beau---at least I thought that for a time.*

Noah was an evangelist who came to Glencoe to hold a tent revival. He was a fiery preacher and turned the whole town to the Lord. He knew the scriptures and spoke eloquently. When he gave a prayer, he looked straight up like he was sending his message right to the Lord God Above. Olieta trembled at his prayers and seeing his beautiful head and eyes uplifted to heaven.

During the three weeks he was in town, he came to the MacTavish home for supper almost every night. Her papa invited him to the first meal, and then he continued to arrive every evening just before supper. They all made jokes about this, and Papa grinned at Olieta and said, "I believe there's somethin' more than supper that keeps that preacher man comin' every night."

Olieta's heart fluttered every time Noah walked up the steps. She made sure to have a fine supper waiting and a big cake for dessert. He enjoyed her cooking and bragged on every dish. She wanted to be near him but spent most of the time getting the meal on the table. He sat by the fire with her parents and sister, Ovieta, who never once offered to help with the meal. That was fine with Olieta because she wanted Brother Noah to know that she had done all the work to serve him his favorite dishes. She knew he grew tired of her silly sister especially during the meal when Ovieta always managed to sit beside him and giggle at everything he said whether it was funny or not. The sisters were identical, but it was not difficult to tell them apart. Ovieta liked to wear bright clothes that Olieta thought unsuitable and often wore her hair long without a braid or bun. Noah being a minister of the Gospel, Olieta knew he did not approve of that.

On the last night of the revival, Olieta went forward at the altar call and gave her heart to the Lord. She had done this long ago as a child but felt the need even more after his sermon. As she headed to the altar, Ovieta followed right behind her. She was glad her sister wanted to get right with the Lord, but Ovieta stood there with a big smile on her face and looked right into the eyes of Brother Noah. *That was no way to act when you were getting saved.*

The next morning Noah came by to say goodbye and vowed to return often.

"Judge MacTavish, I'd like to have a few words with you if you have time."

"Of course, I will be glad to speak with you." Papa thought he would probably ask for a donation to his ministry which Papa would gladly contribute. The girls left the room but stood beside the door hoping to hear the discussion.

"Judge MacTavish, I want to thank you for opening your home to me. I am truly sorry to be leaving, but my ministry calls me to move on. You have two lovely daughters, and I was humbled to have them come to the altar at my last service. I hope to return whenever I am near Glencoe, and I would like your permission to call on your daughter'"

Papa was not surprised, and he was quite happy for Olieta. With a twinkle in his eye, he replied, "You are more than welcome to our home and have my permission to call on my daughter."

"Sir, I am honored to have yore permission to call on Ovieta."

Olieta did not wait to hear Papa's reply and hurried into the bedroom she shared with her sister. Her body shook with anger at what she considered a betrayal. *How could she take the only thing I had ever desired away from me? I have spent my life giving in to what she wants. I always thought this made her love me.*

Ovieta did not return to their room until the buggy drove away. She walked in as though she expected Olieta to be happy for her. *It's just like her to expect me to make her a dress to wear on their first outing.*

"Sister, are you awake. I have so much to tell you."

Olieta pretended to be napping and did not respond. *How could he choose silly, childish Ovieta over me?*

The hope of a future as the wife of a preacher was gone. *I could have helped him so much with the music, the ladies' gatherings and took care of him so he could spend all his time doing the Lord's work. Ovieta can't and won't do anything but try to look pretty.*

There were no tears left to fall. Along with her broken heart came a feeling of total emptiness. The love she had felt for her sister ended at that moment.

Noah came to court Ovieta often, and wedding talk was being whispered. It was hard for Olieta to pretend to welcome him each time he came. Pride would not allow her to do otherwise.

Two weeks before the date set for the wedding, Ovieta caught the fever that was spreading throughout the county. The doctor did everything he knew to break the fever which kept rising. Mama had just given birth to James a few weeks before, so as always, it fell to Olieta to take care of her twin, but not once did she pray for her recovery.

Ovieta died on the third day of the sickness. Noah did not get to her bedside in time. He was devastated during the funeral. After leaving the gravesite, he drove away in his buggy.

They never saw or heard from him again.

As time went on, Olieta's only love was her baby brother, James, and pride for the praise she received for "being strong and upholding the MacTavish name". The townsfolks and even her family all proclaimed that losing her twin sister had changed Olieta into a bitter and desolate woman. Only she knew the truth; she was glad that Ovieta had died, and she did not have to watch her living a life with the man who was meant for her. Acknowledging these feelings made her even more embittered and saddened. Her only joy came from her little brother, James and knowing that he would always love and need her.

Now she had someone else to deal with. James was hers and hers only. *This half-breed interloper from the Washington County trash don't stand a chance with me, Olieta MacTavish, one of the most respected ladies in Glencoe.*

The coming days were not as Olieta expected. Myra brought change to the MacTavish home and seemed to fit right into the household. She cooked meals which the family enjoyed, and Olieta refused to touch. Mama bragged on her ironing and needlework. James beamed and spent every moment with her when he was not at work. No one even objected when she sat on the back steps to talk and laugh with Rosa, the colored girl who lived down the road.

Olieta bided her time and watched Myra's body closely. She could always recognize the signs of pregnancy before it was announced. *The gal's breasts are already tight against her shirtwaist and her belly'll pop out soon. Then James and all would know how she had fooled him into marrying her after she has a little bastard on the way.*

This did not happen. Eleven months after their marriage, Myra gave birth to a baby girl. Olieta had planned to ignore this baby even if the timing meant it was likely James's child.

Myra went off to be with her folks a few times. There's still more than a good chance it ain't his. Gals like her don't know what a marriage vow means.

James had moved Myra into a new house down the road before time for the birth, and Olieta was thankful to have her out of the MacTavish home place. James was a pet of the entire family, and all were excited as they waited for the birth of his first born. Olieta did not share their elation, but she was eager to get a look at the newborn and pronounce that it did not have MacTavish blood.

Early one frosty fall morning, Rosa, the colored girl, came running up the lane shouting, "It's a comin'. Miz Myra done giving birth. Mr. James said for y'all to come on down there."

Papa had already left for his office, but Mama and Olieta hurried down the road. The doctor's buggy was parked in front of the house. Olieta was expecting to hear Myra carrying on like a wild woman as the pains hit. *She doesn't have the dignity not to make a fool of herself.*

James was pacing back and forth on the porch and lighting one cigarette after another. He took a few puffs and then stomped out only to light another. Olieta had never seen her brother so nervous. No sound was coming from the bedroom, and that was strange.

"Son, you sit in the rocker and settle down. It's gonna be over soon. I peeked in and Dr. Yeoman said she is doing fine. Now I'm goin' to see if I can be of help. Olieta, you make some coffee."

Olieta tiptoed past the bedroom to the kitchen and heard only small moans from Myra and reassuring talk from her mother and the doctor. Just as she brought the coffee out for James, her mama came out and said, "James, come into the room and meet yore beautiful daughter."

"It's a girl. That's just what I wanted." He hurried to the room and Olieta was left alone on the porch with her thoughts. *Little girl...huh...little squaw.*

Finally, Mama came out to the porch and invited Olieta to come in and see her new niece. She hesitantly went into the room.

James was sitting on the bed beside Myra as she nursed the baby. He kept saying, "Just look at her. She's the prettiest little thing I've ever laid eyes on. Her name's Idella—Idella Frances MacTavish." He kissed her on the forehead and said, "Today's yore birthday, Idella."

When the nursing ended, James picked the baby up, wrapped her in a pink shawl and brought her over to his sister. Olieta felt her body lock. She could not reach out for the baby and confirm what she was expecting to see. She did not want to break her brother's heart with what she must tell him.

"Take her, Olieta, I want Idella her to meet her aunt right now."

The shawl wrapped infant filled her arms and made a soft cry. Olieta looked into the tiny face, and bright little eyes looked back at her. She reached to uncurl a little finger which latched onto her finger. *Tiny now but I can see the fingers of a piano player. I will teach her to play hymns and teach her how to be a MacTavish and be dignified and prideful of the name. Pore little thing will need her auntie to teach her the ways of a lady. Her ignorant ma shore won't be able.*

Olieta felt a surge through her body. The love that drained from her so many years ago seemed to fill her veins.

Myra would continue to be her nemesis. That would never change, but it was no fault of this tiny little one. There was no denying that this little baby girl was a MacTavish, and Olieta would cherish her forever.

Father and Son

Martin Stuart wiped the sweat from his brow and rested on his hoe as he looked down the cotton row. "Lord, help me, how has it come to this? His gaze took in the stooped backs of his children, diligently chopping out the weeds surrounding the little cotton plants striving to break through the soil.

The battle between the cotton and weeds was continual from the day the seeds were dropped until the last picking. Without this daily back-breaking drudgery, the weeds would triumph and leave the family destitute. The partial wage earned by a sharecropper raising a cotton crop was the only means of a roof over their heads and meager rations for their bellies.

On the day young Martin turned his back and walked out of the door of his family's home, he would not have believed that the time would come when his children would be working in the cotton patch instead of being in school and enjoying the life he had known as a boy. He had no alternative, for raising a cotton crop took much labor, and the only labor he could supply was that of his own and his children.

One by one, his children joined him in the field. Their education and childhood stopped on that day. He could stomach seeing his two boys in the field, but his heart broke on the day he had to tell his beloved little daughter Myra that she too was needed in the field.

The children never resisted. This was the only life they had ever known. He was proud that they were good workers and got through the day by singing, laughing and joking together.

Joe Wiley, the oldest boy, had a harsh way about him and often took out his frustration on the younger children. Papa could understand his feelings of martyrdom and resentment at having no life other than working in the field. Becoming a bully elevated his feelings about himself. Martin often needed to chastise his son, but he never whipped him.

He would not lift a hand to his children. He knew that his wife, Ann, often whipped them too hard and for even the smallest infractions. This never happened when he was present, and the children did not complain to him. It caused him much distress, but he did not admonish her.

She had been raised in the ways of the Creeks and treated her children as she had been treated. He often wondered, *Was it wrong to take her away from her own people even if I did feel I couldn't live without her?* He still hungered at the sight of her and thought her as beautiful as the day he first laid eyes on her although the years had not been kind to her. She had birthed seven babies, passed three before they developed enough to be born, and struggled to keep her wits about her. Her mind was troubled, and he was helpless when she went into depressions that kept her from taking care of the children and unaware of their needs. *Thank you, God, for my little Myra. She has filled in for her ma when she was just a baby herself.*

Martin and his oldest son often had harsh words, and one-day Joe Wiley just walked away to find a better life. This made the need for another hand in the field even more critical.

The night before sending Myra to the field he had prayed, *Lord, I know I've made some wrong turns in my life, but I've always tried to do what I believed was right. Now, please, let me find a way to let my little girl keep on being a little girl and not a field hand. I'll work my hands till they bleed if I can just keep her in school.*

The answer did not come, and the next morning Myra picked up a hoe instead of her school books and lunch bucket.

Martin's papa was a large land owner and raised a cotton crop with the help of sharecroppers. Martin and his younger brother were taught to work and do their share, but their schooling always came first. His papa expected his oldest son to be prepared to assume the responsibility of increasing the production of the farm and keeping the family legacy profitable.

Martin embraced this opportunity for his future. Papa impressed upon his sons that education and learning was the way to increase their inheritance. He told them you must "work smarter, not harder."

By the end of his school years, Martin was well prepared. He had led his class and was viewed by all as a tribute to his family. Martin and his papa had long talks and agreed that before moving into the family business, he would benefit from courses at a new state agricultural school and gain new experiences. At the commencement program of his final year in the local school, Martin gave the address for the class and was recognized as the highest-achieving student. His life was set on a course to become a successful landowner and a leader in his community.

When he boarded the train to head to the college one hundred miles from his home, he was excited and proud of his accomplishments. The two years of college were beneficial, and he returned home ready to step into the role assigned to him. He was thinking of marriage to his school sweetheart who was now a teacher. The family approved and gave their blessings.

During the first week after his return home, he had gone to the general store to purchase work clothes. As he stood and chatted with the store owner, a grizzly looking man and younger boy came into the store and started looking over the counters.

"Excuse me, Martin, I have to keep an eye on them injuns. They'll steal me blind if I don't. Seems like there's always somma that bunch passing through."

From the looks of the newcomers, Martin could understand his concern. The smell of unwashed bodies, wood smoke and liquor permeated the air as they walked around the store. The store owner watched as they picked up a few items.

"Y'all find what ya want and then get on outta my store. I don't allow injuns hanging around, scaring off the customers."

The boy balled his fist ready to swing, but Martin walked between and said, "It's best that you pay for your stuff and move on. I know you don't want trouble."

Martin was relieved when the boy lowered his fists, picked

up his bundle and followed the older man out of the door, but he had a queasy feeling in his gut and didn't want to stand there and talk about what had just happened.

He walked outside and watched as they got onto a rickety old wagon with a heavy load, pulled by a mule that looked in its last days. Sitting on the floor of the wagon were a woman and a young girl who looked about sixteen or so. His eyes could not leave the sight of the young girl. Even in her primitive surroundings and dress, she was the most beautiful girl he had ever seen. He stood in the street and watched until the wagon was out of sight and wondered where they were headed.

When he returned home, his papa met him on the porch and gave an order. "I just saw a wagonload of injuns pass on the road headed towards the creek. You get right down there and run 'em off if they try to camp. In one night, they can steal every animal we own. Take a gun and scare 'em good." He handed Martin a shot gun and did not wait for a reply.

The creek was a few miles away from the house but on land owned by his father. Martin saddled his horse and hoped with all his heart that the Indians would not be at the creek. He did not want to have to tell them to leave—but he also wanted to have one more sight of the girl.

He recognized the wagon. It was unloaded and a make-shift tent had been set up with other items scattered around the creek bank. His eyes were drawn to the figure of the girl drawing water from the creek. They had picked an ideal spot to set up camp. There was clear running water, grass for the mule, and shade from the sun.

He approached the girl at the creek. "Let me help you fill these buckets. I saw you in town today. Where are y'all headed?"

Her coal black hair hung loose to her shoulders and her dark eyes looked like those of a frightened fawn. She shrugged to indicate that she did not know.

"I'm Martin. What is your name?"

She hesitated before speaking. This white man was surely there to make them move on or worse to call the law. She didn't know why but Indians were never welcomed in any of the places they tried to find a home. Her papa was a white man but he had taken up with her ma and to Indian ways. He had told her that most of the Indians had been moved to a land far away and that the white folks wanted all of them gone. *This white man don't look like he's mad 'cause we're here*, she thought.

"My pa's name's Block, and he named me Ann Block. My ma calls me Willow."

"What do you like to be called?" Martin asked as he took the two water buckets to carry.

"It don't matter, 'cause nobody ever calls me. Are you gonna make us move on?"

"No, not until you are ready to leave and if you follow the rules that I tell your pa."

Martin walked up to the wagon area and faced a man twice his size, who was sneering at him with suspicion.

"How do you do, sir. I am Martin Stuart, and my family owns this land where you are camping. This is a pleasant place with plenty of clear, fresh water. It is a good place to rest for a while, but I know you do not plan to stay long."

The man answered with hatred in his stare. "Why didn't yore pa come to run us off 'steada sending his young'un to do the ungodly thing?"

"Sir, my papa is a good man. If he knows you are only here for a short time, and if you don't do any damage or cause a ruckus, I feel that he will allow you to stay."

"Is that the truth or it just a way to get me arrested?"

"No sir, I promise that won't happen as long as you follow the rules I told you."

"Well, I be dammed. I ain't never met a dirt farmer yet who looked on me like a man and not a stray dog. I'm just as white as you, boy. I took up with injuns cause they treated me better than any white folks I'd ever known."

Martin did not want to continue the talk, and he had to think up a way to tell his papa that they were not leaving. He had never disobeyed his papa in his life, but he could not find it in his heart to treat the girl and her family badly.

The girl had watched him during the encounter with her papa. Before striding his horse, he walked over to her. "Miss Ann, I am glad you will be here for a while. I'm comin' back to do some fishin' in the creek. Those little fish taste mighty good when you fry up a bunch."

His papa met him as he put up his horse. *What to say without telling an outright lie.* Not many folks passed down by their creek, so he hoped papa would not even know they were staying.

"Did you get rid of 'em? I didn't hear no gun shot."

"They gonna be leaving." Martin did not tell a lie. He just did not say *when* they were leaving. Papa seemed satisfied.

For the next few weeks, Martin slipped away to the creek every afternoon. He could not stay away from Ann. They held hands to walk in the woods and swam in the creek, and she told him tales of the Indians' hardships which made him sad. It seemed natural to lay close together on the creek bank, but Martin was finding it hard to part from her. The first time he shyly brushed her cheek with his lips, she pulled his mouth down to her lips and gave him a kiss that told him he had to find a way for her to stay with him.

I will catch hell from papa when he learns I did not make them leave—but maybe when I tell him that I love her and want her to stay here with me, he'll understand.

Martin did not have time to appeal to his papa. After three weeks, he went for his afternoon visit and found the wagon being loaded to move on. He could not let her leave and never see her again. But first, he had to face his papa.

After listening to the beginning of Martin's confession, his papa interrupted by holding up his palm and shaking his head vigorously.

"No more, I will hear no more. You have never before disobeyed me and now..."

Martin waited for the rest and knew they would not be easy words to hear.

"First you lied to me and kept the lie going. Now you tell me that you want to take up with a bunch of filthy, shiftless, thieving injuns. I won't have it, and I'm the one taking the shotgun to run 'em off this time. I'd call the sheriff, but they'd tell him what you done—not that he'd believe a worthless injun."

"Papa, first of all they're not worthless or any of the things you called them. They are human beings just like you and me. I believe you and most white folks treat them that way because of shame in how we have taken all their land and left them with nowhere to go. If I was an injun I'd feel the same way."

"You done fell under the spell of that little injun whore. There's plenty more of what you're gettin', Son, you'll find out. There's men who have fallen under the spell of a squaw. They're called squaw men and doin' that makes 'em less than an injun. It's a sin and an abomination before the Lord God to breed outside of yore own sort. You better pray, boy. Lying to yore papa is bad, but what you've done is worse."

Martin's mouth filled with bile, and he hoped he could keep from vomiting. The words had cut like a knife, and his heart was shattered. The one man in all the world that he believed to be fair and just had shown his feet of clay. *What will come next?* Martin thought for a moment. *No matter, I have to defend the one I love.*

"Papa, it ain't like that with Ann. I want her to be my wife, and I hoped your daughter-in-law. The only thing I've done wrong is lie to you. I can't take the time to defend myself or argue about yore hurtful words. I've gotta get to the creek before they leave. I cannot let her go. I must say that I heard somewhere that God loves us all—I think I heard that in church. Now I have to go. "

"If you leave now, don't ever show yore face here again, Squaw Man. To me, yore mama, brother, and sister you are as dead as if I put a bullet in yore heart. I'll give you one thing, and that's yore horse, 'cause I want you away from here as quick as you can go."

"Goodbye, Papa. I will always love you and my family, but I cannot give up the woman I love."

Martin's horse was still saddled after his ride home from the creek. He climbed astride, geed the horse ahead and did not look back. His mama and sister stood in the road and watched him ride out of their life.

Schoolmarm

Miss Caroline stood in the freezing cold on the little stoop of the schoolhouse and pulled the rope to ring the bell announcing the start of the schoolday. She was a schoolmarm, a teacher in a one-room rural school. This was the first school day after Christmas holidays, and she was excited to see the children.

As expected, many of the students were absent. All walked to and from school, and many homes were often several miles away. Being absent on such a cold day was excusable. However, no matter what the weather, the children were often absent for the necessity of helping with the farm work. Few parents could afford to do without the labor of their children.

The one-room school was situated at a crossroads and served students from every direction. There was no town nearby, and the school was provided by the few parents who were able to pay a small amount and a wealthy landowner who was childless.

No child was turned away, but the students started leaving permanently about age thirteen.

Miss Caroline was the sole teacher of all levels of students. It was her mission to teach them as much as possible during the days they were in school.

The cold air was whipping around her dress and chapping her cheeks, so she gave the last pull of the rope and was ready to start the schoolday. The pot-bellied stove in middle of classroom was warm and inviting.

Before she turned, three little figures appeared trudging up the road. A closer look revealed a girl and two small boys. They were coming to school.

She had not expected new students. *Wonder how far they have walked,* she thought. *The pore little things must be freezing.*

In a small, meek voice the little girl said, "Marm, we've come to go to school. I know we'se late but it was a longer walk than we 'spected."

"Well, you come right in and get warmed up. How far have you walked?"

"We live on Mr. Clyde's place. We just moved there from over close to Bartow."

"Yes, I know Mr. Clyde Bennett." *Dear Lord, that is over two miles, and this little one can't be more than six. All three are thin as a rail. I'm thankful they are with the Bennetts. They're good folks.*

"Here's a paper my papa sent that tells ya who we is."

They were now inside and warming by the fire. The other students started snickering and whispering about the new students. "They so pore they lucky to have a hickory nut and a rock to crack it in their lunch bucket."

Grady, a boy who was usually rowdy, caused a loud laugh

and more comments from several others.

"That will be enough of that talk, Grady," said Miss Caroline. "You have just won the job of filling the wood box for the next two weeks." The class became silent.

Miss Caroline's heart cringed. The children were clean, but their clothes were shabby and not nearly adequate for such a cold day. She started to read the note and was surprised to find it legible—which was not usually true of notes from parents.

> *Dear Schoolmarm,*
>
> *My children will be attending your school for the remainder of the term. They are smart children and mind well, but behind in their learning because of lack of opportunity to go to school regularly. It is my hope that they can finish this year in your class. Their information follows:*
>
> *Myra Frances Stuart is 12 years old. She is very bright and a hard worker. I pray you will have patience in helping her learn.*
>
> *Arno Jefferson Stuart is 8 years old. He doesn't talk much, but I can tell that learning comes easy to him.*
>
> *Jesse Stanley Stuart is six years old. I admit that he is a handful but means no harm. You feel free to discipline him as needed.*
>
> *Thank you, Marm, for taking care of my children,*
> *Martin Stuart*

Looking at the three little waifs before her and reading the well-written, perfectly spelled and punctuated note was confusing. The vocabulary was of an educated man—not a sharecropper. *Who was this father who had neglected his children's education and even their clothing and feeding?*

She was a teacher, and her job was to teach children to the upmost of their abilities. Her heart had broken more than once at the pitiful plight of the sharecropper children who made up the majority of her class—but these children were different.

It was impossible to spend much time with any one student when she had to teach everyone from the youngest to the most advanced. Today, she had to make time for these new students who seemed so lost and unprepared.

Jesse was occupied immediately when she handed him a bag of alphabet blocks. His eyes sparkled, and he handled the blocks with care. Later, she would use the blocks to teach him the alphabet.

Arno hungrily reached for the Blue-Back Speller and became absorbed with the majesty of words. Caroline felt a rush of excitement to watch him become one with the book. It hadn't happened often in Miss Caroline's career that she found a student to challenge her teaching skills. Moments like this told her that teaching came from her heart.

Now, to Myra. Despite her shabby appearance she was as beautiful a child as the teacher had ever seen. It was very evident that she had inherited Indian characteristics, which gave her skin the color of coffee with rich cream. Her hair was black as a raven. Jesse had the same dark skin and hair, but he did not have the radiance of his sister. Arno did not look Indian at all. He was blond and fair with hazel eyes.

Myra seemed to freeze when the textbook was placed in her hands, and as soon as the teacher turned, she put the book back on the teacher's desk.

She was assigned a seat with the older students. For the rest of the morning she sat in the classroom trying to make sense out of what the teacher was saying about how people had come across the water to settle this country. She couldn't figure out why they would cross the water to come to these woods.

No mention was made of the Indians coming with them. *Maybe they were already here.*

Miss Caroline clanged the bell for dinner time. "The day has warmed up enough for you to go outside to eat your lunches, but if your coats are not warm enough, you may stay inside to eat." She added the last words when she remembered how cold the three new students had been when they had arrived.

Myra brought out their lunch bucket and herded her brothers to the far corner of the playground to eat their dinner.

The teacher watched as the little girl opened the bucket and broke up biscuits for the three to share. As she ate her lunch, the piece of cold chicken, the cheese and the slice of apple pie she had eaten seemed to stick in her chest.

On the way back to the schoolroom, Myra spied a long piece of white string under the board steps. She could find a use for anything, so she made sure no one was watching and retrieved the string from under the step. The afternoon was even of less interest to her than the tale of settlers crossing the water. This was the time for reciting and reading from the Blue

Back Speller. She was never called forward, but surprisingly Arno took his turn when called and recited a list of words.

Miss Caroline intentionally passed her by since she recognized that Myra had not opened the book and was absorbed in tying a string into a design. The schoolmarm watched as Myra's little hands made a series of perfectly spaced knots in the string. *How can I reach her? How can I use that ability to use her hands to learn other skills? I know she can learn.*

For the rest of the school day and throughout her evening at home, Caroline could not stop thinking. *There must be a way— there must be a way.*

Hoping to clear her thoughts and relax before trying to sleep, she took out her crocheting and put more stitches into a shawl she was making for her aunt. The clicking of the needles gave her satisfaction—and also an answer.

I will teach her to crochet. From that I can lead her to counting and numbers. Reading can come from simple directions I will write. Not all children learn in the same way, and this does not mean they are limited. If a child can't learn the way I teach—then I must teach the way they can learn.

She could hardly wait for the next day and packed a bag with extra needles, thread, and a few finished pieces of crocheting to show the child.

Myra spent the next morning intrigued with changing designs using the string. She had decided the schoolmarm had forgotten her, or maybe she was relieved that her new student was occupied with anything.

Before pulling the rope to announce dinner time, Miss Caroline squatted down beside Myra at her desk. "Myra, could you stay inside with me to eat your dinner. I'm sure Arno can help Jesse, and they will be fine without you."

Myra could only nod her head as she squeezed her eyes to hold back the tears. Her oldest brother had taught her to do this when Ma whipped her. *Had Miss Caroline already decided that she was too dumb to be in school?*

The dinner bell rang, and Myra opened the lunch pail and brought out her biscuit. There were a few slices of sweet potato, also, but she left that in the pail for her brothers to take outside.

Miss Caroline placed a little basket covered with cloth on top of her desk. Myra watched curiously as her teacher spread out the cloth and placed her food on it. *I never thought about schoolmarm's eatin' but I guess they do whatever we do.* She did not want to take that thought any further.

"Oh, my, Mother has packed too much for me to eat," said Miss Caroline. "She always thinks I should eat more. I hate to throw it away, and if I take it back home, she will be disappointed. Would you help me eat some of this food, Myra?"

Myra had already choked down her cold dry biscuit and her throat was parched for water. "Yessum, I'll try if ya ain't hongry fer all of it."

"Then, first, go to the well and get yourself a big dipper of water. I know you are thirsty after this long morning with nothing to drink."

"Do ya want me to bring ya a dipperful?"

"No, dear, my mother packed a bottle of tea for me." Miss Caroline began placing the divided lunch on both ends of the cloth. Myra's eyes got big and her mouth watered when she saw that each had a hard-boiled egg, a biscuit spread with butter and jam, and an apple.

"Marm, this is more than enough fer me. Can I give this biscuit to my brothers? They shore love somethin' sweet." There was no way for her to enjoy this feast without sharing with her brothers.

Miss Caroline smiled as she shook her head. "No, Myra, but you can give them these," and she handed over a sack with two of the same butter and jam biscuits. "Remind them to drink a dipper of water and to use the outhouse before I ring the bell to end dinner time."

Myra raced out to the far end of playground but peeped into the bag before giving to the boys. She saw two apples along with the biscuits. Her heart leaped knowing the joy the apples would bring. Christmas was the only time they had apples and not even every Christmas.

After finishing the meal, Miss Caroline said, "Hold up your head, Myra, and look at me."

"Yessum."

"Myra, I have noticed how well you work with your hands. I have a new assignment I think will be more beneficial for you to learn."

Myra trembled at the thought that the teacher had already found her too dumb to learn schoolwork. She feared the new assignment would be lining up the alphabet blocks with Jesse.

The teacher went to her desk and brought out a cloth bag. Myra wanted to run out of the schoolhouse and hide before she was shamed in front of the whole class. She loudly caught her breath and let out a sigh of relief when a long shiny needle and a ball of white thread was removed from the bag along with scarves and squares made from different colors of thread.

Miss Carolina displayed several of the pieces of the needlework across the desktop and said, "Myra, these have been made by crocheting. I think you would be good at this. Would you like for me to teach you?"

"Oh, yessum. I want to learn that more than I have ever wanted anythang in my life."

The teacher gave Myra a needle and ball of thread. Both started working, and Myra followed each stitch. At first her fingers did not work any better with the needle than they did with a pencil, but she quickly got the hang of making a stitch. Soon, she was making a row of stitches.

Miss Caroline clapped her hands and hugged Myra. "I have to ring the bell for the others to come inside. I'm afraid I gave them a longer time for dinner. Take this bag with your needle and thread and keep practicing when you get home. We will work more tomorrow during dinner time."

For the next few weeks teacher and student crocheted through the dinner recess every day, and Myra's skill increased. She worked fast and accurately, and her stitches were tight and straight. Crocheting gave her a feeling of elation that she had never felt before. And the schoolmarm's mother continued to pack too much lunch for her daughter to eat.

What a thrill to see this child learn a skill and show such enjoyment, thought Miss Caroline. *This is the fulfillment that made me become a teacher. Now I can teach her much more. Next, we will learn numbers by counting stitches and then maybe on to reading word cards.*

Miss Caroline always planned to be a teacher. She struggled to find the means to go away to Normal School for a year. One year of normal school qualified her to teach in a one-room school where the pay was minimal. Little jobs at the school and the mite her parents could contribute enabled her to attend for one year. Her father's death brought her home to help her mother run the small farm with the aid of an elderly black family who had lived on their place for as long as she could remember.

When she got the teaching position in the little one-room school near her home, she was ready to share the magic of learning with all her students. Sadly, this did not happen often because of lack of motivation, interference from farm work, and difficulty filling the needs of so many children.

Then along had come Myra. Miss Caroline left the classroom each day with excitement and renewed love and faith in teaching. She welcomed each new schoolday, and her thoughts were consumed with approaches to use with this eager and gifted learner.

On a morning in early March, the schoolmarm watched the children trudging up the path to the school. One by one, she identified each student and noticed any absentees. *There's Jesse and Arno, but where is Myra?*

"Good morning, boys, where is your sister? I hope she's not sick."

Arno spoke in his meek, quiet tone, "No'um, she ain't sick, but she can't come to school no mo."

Stunned, Miss Caroline asked, "You mean today, this week or how long?"

The younger one, Jesse, spoke out. "Never, she ain't never goin' to school no mo."

"Arno, I thought she loved school!" exclaimed Miss Caroline.

Tears ran down the little boy's face. "She do. She love school but our papa need her to work in the field. There ain't no way we can keep ahead of the weeds if she don't help with the choppin."

Tears flooded the teacher's eyes, and she gathered both boys in an embrace. "Tell her I will miss her and to keep on with her crocheting."

The schoolmarm felt some hope. *This child may never have a chance to attend school again—but the door to learning has been opened to her.*

That is the tale of a country schoolmarm and the education of a sharecropper's child.

Sisters

James sat on the edge of the bed and examined his newborn daughter. "Myra, I swear she's just as pretty a baby as her sister. I shore am proud, and I down right thank you for another little daughter. Now, what we gonna name her?"

"I thought you wuz wantin' a boy, and I already had the name in mind." Myra was thankful that he wasn't disappointed with a second girl, but she should have known better. James was not the kind of man to be partial.

"So how about Lizzie Nell, Gertie Faye or Nannie Bessie like yore aunt you speak so highly of?" joked James.

"I don't think any one of those suit her. I wanted to name a boy for you, but I'll have to wait on that." She knew James would have a name in mind that would sound much nicer than the old timey names most folks named their children.

"Well, I done picked out Laura. How's that sound to ya?" This time James was sincere.

"How 'bout Laura James? When you put the two names together, it sounds really pretty and suits her fine."

The name felt right to Myra's ear. James grinned from ear to ear. "Ma, come on in here and meet Laura James MacTavish."

His mother had been waiting to allow her son to have alone time with his wife and new daughter. The doctor had told Mrs. MacTavish all about her fine new granddaughter as he was leaving the house.

James put the baby girl into his ma's arms with joy. "Tell Olieta and Idella we are ready for them to come in too."

"They're back at my house, son, but I'll send Rosa to get them. She has been sittin' on the front steps waiting for the birth. You know how much she loves Myra."

"Send her to get 'em. I wanted Idella to stay here to come in and see the baby right away. Why did Olieta go home?"

"You know how Olieta thinks. She thought Idella should not be here until the baby was already born and cleaned up. She was afraid Idella would start to wonder about where babies come from."

"Hell, where does she want the child to think they come from—the cabbage patch?"

"I wouldn't doubt that, but that's yore sister, and she's not gonna change. I think I hear them comin' in the front door."

Olieta was eager to see her new niece, but she feared making Idella feel less special since a new baby had come. She also had to come up with some answers if the child asked where the baby came from. Myra had told the little innocent thing that a baby was growing in her stomach and even let her feel it move. *That is just plain trashy and nothing a child needs to know. I hope I can erase those nasty thoughts out before she starts talking about it*. Olieta thought everything about the human body should be kept secret. Every time her sisters talked about such things, she excused herself from the room.

"Look at her, Olieta. She's just as fine as her sister. I shore am proud to be their papa." James placed the shawl-wrapped newborn in the arms of his sister.

"She's a nice plump baby all right, but she does not look a bit like a MacTavish."

This was true. Laura James favored her mother, which pleased James.

"I can see injun likeness in her. Her skin will be dark and not pretty and white like our darling, Idella. Take the baby back to Myra, James. Idella and I need to go back to the house."

"No ma'am, our *darling* Idella ain't goin' nowhere. She's home to stay with me, her mama and baby sister. Come on, *darlin'*, let's go watch yore mama feed Laura James. Then you might can hold her." James' voice showed his anger when he emphasized the word darling.

Olieta went home in a huff. *It will be up to me to help Idella rise above the raising she's won't be getting. Left up to Myra, both of them will be running like wild savages—the way she was raised. I plan to show this new one attention and not make a difference in them, but it will try my patience.*

The years flew by, the children grew, and a baby boy was added to the family. When Idella started to school, she walked home every afternoon with the other MacTavish children.

Most of the family lived on the same road. Olieta felt it was her responsibility to call Idella from the group and share the benefits of knowing proper behavior for a MacTavish.

"Come over and sit with Auntie for a while, precious. We will have our tea time together. "

Idella gladly ran over and knew she would be getting a soda water and cookies. Besides the treats, she loved hearing the praise her aunt always poured on her.

"Now you tell me about your day at school. I know you are the top one in the class and you're certainly the prettiest."

"Yessum, I do make the best marks, but some of the others don't like me for that."

"Of course, they don't like you showing them up. They can't help not being smart like you. One thing you must always remember when you have to deal with such—You are a MacTavish. Hold your head up—stand straight—and be proud of it."

"I'll always do that, Auntie. It's better to be a MacTavish, ain't it?"

"Isn't it—don't you let their ignorance rub off on you. Yes, The MacTavishes are thought more highly of than most folks around here."

"What about Laura James? Ain't—I mean isn't she a MacTavish?"

"Don't fret about her. We'll talk about that another time."

Throughout their school years, Laura James walked in the footprints of her big sister. She tried to keep up, but she could never pass her. At age ten, Idella could play the piano, to her aunt's delight. She played church hymns and tunes of songs she had only heard. She was as neat in her dress as the aunt who adored her. Another baby sister had now joined the family, but Idella remained the pride and joy of her papa and her aunt.

"James, that girl is more MacTavish than me and you put together. She's smart, talented, sweet as an angel and pretty as a doll." Olieta always reminded her brother of this as his family grew.

"Now sister, are you sayin' that me and you ain't pretty and sweet?" James always tried to make a joke when Olieta said this. But he did not like to hear his eldest put ahead of her sisters and brother.

All children were different, and that did not make one better than the other. However, he shared his sister's pride and beamed when Idella played the piano at church, looking so pretty in a new dress her mama had made.

Laura James usually trailed behind her mama and was her helper. She could clean up the kitchen as good as a grownup and watched her mama to learn about cooking. Myra felt at ease to leave the two younger ones in her care.

Myra spent most of her time sewing after her chores were done. Idella loved new dresses, and Myra's outfits looked better than store-bought. That was one thing she could do for her oldest that satisfied the girl.

Idella had a harshness that could cut Myra to the core, especially when she criticized Laura James. Besides her criticism of her sister, she often lashed out at her mama. "Why don't you try to talk better. You sound dumb and ignorant when you say 'hit' for 'it' and 'thems' for 'they' and 'yore' for "your." And if you'd cut your hair, you'd look much neater."

Myra never commented. She knew who was putting these thoughts into her daughter's head.

Through their school years, the MacTavish girls were the best dressed in their class—thanks to Myra's sewing skills. Being only two years apart, Laura James was the right size for hand-me-downs from her sister. The dresses were always in perfect condition for a second user.

Laura James never complained. She was as proud of a hand-me-down as a brand-new dress. Actually, she felt proud to wear her sister's clothes. Myra always planned to make a dress especially for Laura James, but she never seemed to catch up with the sewing for Idella.

Laura James could claim one asset over her sister. Since babyhood, her head had been covered with naturally curly ringlets. Idella learned to put her hair up with rags at night which gave a little curl and looked nice, but she secretly resented her sister's curls.

She claimed to have seen her sister admiring her curls in a mirror and proclaiming, "I'm pretty and what makes me deny it." Taunting Laura James was her pleasure, and when her sister heard this remark, it led to a fight between the two.

One day, James surprised Myra. "Our oldest is gettin' to be a young lady. She'll be sixteen on her birthday next week. I want to buy her something special to show how proud we are of her."

James had never mentioned a present before. When Myra became sixteen, she was already married and Idella was on the way. "I always make a cake for the young'uns on their birthdays. Ain't that enough?"

She thought about it again. Maybe it would be a good thing to get her a present. *I am proud that she has turned out so well and will finish school this year—even if she does have a lot of ways like Olieta.*

James stood in the door. "Come ride to the drugstore and help me pick out something."

It was always a treat for Myra to take a ride with James without all the young'uns in the car. Enjoying a ride with James made her think of their courting days when they rode in a buggy instead of a car.

Inside the drugstore, Myra had no notion of what to even look for as a present. James searched up and down the counter cases, and then said, "That's what I want. Dr. Davis, let me see that gold compact."

When James handed Myra the small, round gold compact, she had no idea of its use. He pushed a little clasp and the lid popped up to show a mirror, a small powder puff, and space for powder. This was the perfect gift for her prissy daughter. She did not even ask James the price, for this was one time that money did not matter.

"We oughta get her some Cody face powder in her shade to go with it." This surprised James because usually Myra raised hell when he spent money on what she called foolishness.

Right then, Myra made up her mind that she would

buy a compact for Laura James on *her* sixteenth birthday. For graduation, all the girl's in Idella's class were to wear white. Myra made her graduating daughter a white linen dress and embroidered roses around the hem.

It was a proud day to see her daughter finish school, which in Myra's life would have been impossible. James believed in keeping his children in school, and he would see that they all finished. He had even talked about sending their son, Stephen, up to Athens to make a doctor or lawyer.

By the end of Laura James' senior year, the Great Depression had enveloped the entire country. James had lost his job and couldn't find any kind of work. Customers stopped coming to Myra for dressmaking. Banks closed and folks lost what money they had.

Myra was thankful for the larder of canned and dried foods she had saved. Every egg the chickens laid was stretched to make a filling meal. Myra protected the hens, but in no time, they had eaten all the roosters but one. She had to keep him around to set eggs for more chicks. Her second daughter's sixteenth birthday passed without notice…and no gold compact.

"Laura James, you know we got no money to buy material to make your graduation dress. I always planned on making one for you as pretty as Idella had."

"I know, Mama, but it can't be helped. I'm just thankful that I could stay in school and graduate. A lot of my class had to drop out and try to find work to help out at home. I just won't go to the ceremony. I will ask my teacher to give my diploma to me on the last day of class."

"No, I can remake Idella's dress to fit you right, and nobody will know it ain't brand new." Myra wasn't much on hugging, but she welcomed the hug and kiss on the cheek from this daughter—who also wasn't much on hugging.

The entire family, including Olieta and Mrs. MacTavish, sat and admired Laura James sitting on the stage with the graduates. Idella made one remark which told her mama how she felt. "Huh, that old dress did turn out okay for her to wear."

Awards were given out for high grades, good attendance and boys that played ball games. The last one was to be the highest honor. Professor Downs and one of the town leaders, Mr. W.L. Dolby, came to the front of the stage.

"Every year we give an award to the senior who throughout their school years has done good work and shown kindness and concern for our school, teachers and students. This year I am proud to award the W.L. Dolby Good Citizenship Medal to Miss Laura James MacTavish. I must also add that this is the first time the faculty has voted one hundred percent for a student."

The entire audience stood to clap as Laura James walked up to receive her certificate and a pin to wear.

Idella never received an award, but she did stand and clap for her sister.

Rosa

"*Lord Jesus, Lord Jesus, y'all take care of Miz Myra. I don't know how much ya listens to prayin' of black folks like me, but wese shore do a heap of hit. Miz Myra done been trying to push out that baby since early this mornin'. She such a little thang and don't know 'bout birthin' babies. Help her. Lord Jesus, if you will. I shore think a heap uv her.*"

Rosa sat on the back steps of the fine, new house Mr. James had built for Miz Myra and him. She was worrying and waiting for her beloved Miz Myra to have her first baby. They had depended on each other since the day Mister James brought her home as his wife. The MacTavish were well-off white folks, but she and Myra were as close as a black and white pair could be.

I done birthed three *of my own already and sho 'member how them babies tore me part getting borned. Granny Etta came ever time, but all she could do to help was put a knife under the bed to cut the pain. Old Doc Youmans done come and gone in with Miz Myra. Wonder if he knows about the knife. It sho don't sound like he's give her no relief.*

Sweat from the early September heat covered Rosa's brow and rolled down into her eyes and made her threadbare dress stick to her body. Her bare toes nervously dug a trench in the dirt under the low step. There wasn't a thing she could do to help.

If'un Granny Etta wuz here she'd be callin' fer me to help. White folks like the MacTavishes don't believe in granny women. Dey calls the doctor. I betcha Granny Etta done brought twice or even three times mo babies into the world as old Doc Youmans.

Miss Olieta came out twice and tried to run her off, but this was one time when Rosa would not obey the cross old lady.

She never heard the baby's first cries, but when Doc Youmans came out of the house and left in his buggy, she knew the baby had been born. Slipping around the house to the front window, she could hear Mister James tell his ma and sister, "We have a fine baby girl."

"*Thank you, Lord Jesus, thank you Lord Jesus. I'm gotta hep Miz Myra take care dis baby.*"

Rosa tried to peep in the window of the Myra's bedroom hoping to get a peek at the baby, but she wasn't tall enough to see over the japonica bush blocking the view.

James called to her through the open window. "Rosa, you come on in here. Myra wants to show you our daughter."

Thank you, Lord Jesus. That Mister James is a carin' man. I'm glad I done see'd Miss Olieta headed to her house rit after Doc Youmans left. She'd never let me get near Miz Myra's baby. I'll wash my hands and feet out here at the well before I goes in.

She went into the house through the back door and eased into the bedroom. James motioned her to come over to the bed where he was cradling the baby in his arms. Rosa could do nothing but grin. "Lordy, Miz Myra, this here's the first newborn white chile I ever see'd. She looks like them little dolls in the windows of the stores at Christmas."

"Rosa, I'll really need yore help. The doctor says I have to stay in bed for two weeks."

"I'll be right here to hep you, Miz Myra. You know you can count on Rosa."

"What about yore baby? She ain't weaned yet. Who will help you?"

"That ain't no trouble. My ma and sister be there to help. I'll just run home when I needs to nurse her."

"Good," said James. "That's all set. You know I'll do right by you, Rosa."

"Yes sir, Mister James, the pay I gets from you is a big hep. My Ezra make a little bit loading the log trucks when he gets the work, but we can't count on that."

"Rosa, you let me know any time I can help y'all out. I know it is a hard scrabble for you to keep yore young'uns fed."

Yes, Lord, that Mister James is one of ya good men, and I thank ya for folks like him and Miz Myra. I ain't met many white folks even care if my young'uns go hungry.

Rosa's own family increased rapidly as well as Myra's family. She continued to walk through the branch every day to see if she could do something for Miz Myra. Often Olieta was there, and sent her away before she had a chance to see Myra.

Lord, Jesus, I do try to pray to think kindly of Miss Olieta, but I can't say that it's workin'. I know she tell Mister James that I come every day 'spectin' to get a handout give to me. Miz Myra do give me a little now and then, but that's come from her good heart. I will keep prayin' 'bout Miss Olieta—but don't 'spect much happenin'.

Years passed, and more babies came for both Myra and Rosa. The fourth baby for Myra was scrawny little thing that came into the world crying and didn't stop except to nurse.

Maybe it's because Mr. James named her Wallace, which didn't seem right for a baby girl. Rosa had trouble calling the little baby girl such an old man's name.

She still got a laugh remembering how she made a "sugar tit" to keep the baby from bawling between feedings. When James didn't hear the bawling every time he came home he told Rosa, "I don't know what the hell a sugar tit is—but you give her all she wants."

When the next baby was born to Rosa she knew the tiny little thing was not right. Seemed like he couldn't get the breath in or out of him. He only lived two days.

As soon as Myra heard of the baby's death, she rushed to her friend. All of Rosa's family had gathered and saw a sight they had never seen before. Miz Myra—and her a MacTavish—bathing the tiny dead infant and dressing him in a gown she had made for her own expected baby. Later, Mister James came in and added to the money needed to bury the baby.

Myra and James' fifth baby girl died after living only six weeks. Rosa was there the night the baby drew her last breath, and it was Rosa who took the baby from her arms and said, "Dis baby girl's one of God's angels now."

A few years later Ezra was at work loading the log trucks. Rosa sent DeWayne, her oldest boy, to where his papa was working. She always sent water and something to eat at dinner time. When he could get work loading the log trucks, he did not stop until all the work was finished.

She could hear her boy hollering long before she could see him. "Ma, Ma, Papa done got hurt. De logs all rolled back on him. Da tryin' to get him out from under all dem logs."

Rosa threw down the wash she had been hanging and ran to the site. When she got there the logs had been removed, and Ezra was being carried to the back of an empty truck. She ran to look at him and knew there was no hope. He was dead. His ribs had been crushed and his lungs were punctured.

Oh Lord Jesus, you gimme as good a man as ever lived and now you took him. I ain't able to read from the Bible, but the preacher tries to tell us that you love us even if we is black. I can't help thinkin' that ya do love us but just not as much as the white folks. Some have told me that you cursed us makin' us black. I got to do me some praying to figure that out. Answer me this one time—tell me how I gonna take care uv my chilluns now that you took Ezra. Amen, Rosa that stays in Glencoe.

She got one answer immediately when Mr. Medlock, the white man who owned the log company, said she could keep living in the little shotgun house on his property for as long as she needed. She would need it for most of the rest of her life.

James put in most of the money needed for Ezra's burying and brought a pair of pants, white shirt and a tie for him to wear when he was laid out for folks to see. Rosa was proud to see her husband looking fit for his burying. *Don't know who Mister James got them clothes from. Couldn't uv been his'un cause Ezra lot bigger man than Mister James.*

Rosa picked up a little work now and then which kept them fed along with keeping a garden, a few laying hens and whatever Myra could give her.

The hard times, called the Great Depression, made it a struggle to survive for white and black alike. Help came from President Roosevelt. He sent food, called commodities, to folks who needed help. Even Myra got her share. *Lord, bless that President Roosevelt,* she prayed.

The prayer she had lifted the day Ezra died continued to trouble her heart. She thought on it every night before she closed her eyes. It took a few years before she could see how the Lord Jesus had cared for her.

Lord Jesus, I been actin' like a poutin' chile ever since my Ezra been gone. Now I have to tell you how 'shamed I am. From what the preacher tells us, you had plenty of hard times in yore life when you wuz one of us. Now I knows you love us black folks just as much as the whites. Bad times come to us, but you send us folks like Mister James and Miz Myra and Mister Medlock, and now even the president of the United States done give me rations to keep my young'uns bellies full. Forgive me Lord Jesus, and I thank ya. Amen, Rosa that stays in Glencoe.

Over the years, a lot of folks in the quarters pestered her with stories about Mister James that she did not want to hear. They tried to convince her that he spent time at junk joints, drinking and hanging around bad women more than a married man should.

I ain't listening to a word of that trash talk. I know Mister James be good to Miz Myra and his chilluns. I sometimes think Miz Myra could brag on him more than she does. I know my Ezra always stood up straighter when I told him how much I thought of him. That isn't her way, but she do keep a good home for him and the chillums. That's all they business and none of mine.

When James died, the pain was almost as much as when she lost Ezra. Rosa helped Myra clean out her house and pack everything into a truck to take to Fitzgerald. She would live there close to her oldest son, Stephen.

I know this is the best thing for Miz Myra. It be hard fer her to get over Mister James' passing. Mister Stephen'll take good care of his mama—but it shore leaves a big hole in my heart.

After James died and Myra left, Rosa started feeling her age. Arthritis crippled her, and there wasn't much she could do. She was blessed to have a daughter and grandchildren to help her. Most of her time was spent sitting on the front porch and thinking back to when Myra was with her almost every day.

A boy drove up in what she recognized as the car of Mrs. Rosenberg, the Jewish lady that ran a store. *He must be lost. I know he don't want nothin' here.*

He had a message from Mrs. Rosenberg—Myra had died. She would be brought home to Glencoe and buried beside James, her angel baby and brother Jesse who was killed in the World War II.

Rosa only thanked him, and then the sobs came. She sobbed until there were no sobs left. She had to be with her Miz Myra one last time. Black folks never knew what to do about going to a gathering of white folks, but she would not let that stop her from saying goodbye to her best friend.

I know how to keep my place and taught my chilluns the same. Miz Myra never had no use for such as makin' black folks move off the street to let whites pass or us always comin' in through the back door. There wuz times when she'd sit right down at the table and eat with me. Not many folks have hearts like Miz Myra.

On the day of the burying, Rosa went to stand by the highway where she knew the hearse would be coming into Glencoe from Fitzgerald. She wasn't alone—the highway was lined with other black folks.

The sheriff's car led the hearse into town. Following the hearse were more cars than she could count. Rosa recognized Mister Stephen and Miz Wallace in one of the cars. Aside from family, a lot of the cars carried folks from Fitzgerald.

"This makes me proud to see Miz Myra honored dis way. Everybody what knew her loved her. Did y'all know that she wuz raised as hard as us and was part injun?"

Every one standing by the road agreed, "Miz Myra wuz one fine lady."

At the gravesite, Myra and her two daughters stood a way back from the crowd of white folks. She listened to the words and prayers said over this dear lady. They had not planned to do anything but listen, but as Myra's casket was lowered into the ground Rosa felt the strains of *Amazing Grace* coming from her lips, and her daughters joined right in.

It was the right thing to do.

Mrs. Rosenberg

Ten-month-old Rachael Rosenberg slept peacefully across her mother's lap. Leah, her mother, nodded and tried to stay awake. She was exhausted from the long train ride from Penn Station in New York City to Savannah, Georgia. The baby was sleeping soundly, but three-year-old Isaac was trying every way he could to free himself from the hold she had on his arm. Like most three-year-old boys, he needed to run around and exert his pent-up energy, but Leah was concerned that he not disturb other passengers.

The long day started when the taxi came to her parent's home in Brooklyn to take Leah, the two children, two trunks and a carry-on bag to Penn Station. The train left at midnight for the trip south. This seemed like the best time to travel with children—she had hopes they would sleep for most of the trip. As the taxi darted through the streets of the only hometown she had every known, misgivings filled her thoughts.

Should I get on this train with my children and head to a place that will be totally foreign to me? I have hardly been away from the neighborhood where I was born.

Mose, Leah's husband, had hoped to someday own a department store, and the chance had come from a distant cousin—in a little town in Georgia called Glencoe.

Mose had gone ahead to open the store. They would live in the back room of the store until a house was found. She was nervous, but she was a strong Jewish woman and a good mate to her husband. She always stood by his side.

She took the same route he had taken, catching a taxi from Brooklyn to Penn Station, and then boarding the "Orange Blossom Special," a fast luxury train that took mainly vacationers from the North to the vacationland of south Florida. Both had made their trips during the late summer—that was the slowest season for the train and economy passage was available.

Also like Mose, she and the children would sleep in their seats. They had not paid the extra to be in a Pullman car. Leah slept so little that it did not matter whether she was—the noise of the rails and bumps and swaying of the train kept her awake.

She spent the night wondering about this journey into the unknown. *How will I make the change to a second train in Savannah? How can I keep my son occupied during the three hours wait and keep the baby from crying?*

Day two of the journey began when the porter came through selling bags of breakfast food. Thoughts of the pot of strong hot coffee that always started her days made her tempted to order a cup from the dining car, but she had to conserve their funds. Her carry-on bag was filled with items to feed the children, but she did purchase a small bottle of milk.

When the sun rose, Leah raised the window curtain and looked out at the passing terrain. There were miles and miles of fields and forests and no city in sight. Occasionally, she saw a group of people in the distance working in a field.

The scene outside the train was green and filled with trees and plants. At first, she thought she was seeing a large park, but it went on for miles and miles. Even Central Park was not this large. As the sun rose higher in the sky, she could make out small towns, but the train did not stop.

It was unnerving to her to look out and see something so different—not to see buildings, hordes of people and sidewalks.

"Next stop is Savannah Georgia. Everyone going to Savannah go to the exit door in the next car forward." A tall black man dressed in the uniform of the railroad shouted over and over. "Mam, get yore bundles and babies and follow me." His soft accent was pleasing to her unaccustomed ear, and she loved the instruction to follow him.

The station in Savannah was small compared to Penn but still confusing. She located a board that told her the train she would need to complete her journey to Glencoe and the time. This train was plainly called "The Seaboard Airline."

Three more hours and we will be on our way to Mose and our new home. Suddenly, she felt excitement rather than fear.

The view from the train window of the Seaboard now showed lush growths of trees and fields of what she first thought was snow—but that couldn't be given the heat she was experiencing on the train. She overheard a fellow passenger call it cotton.

The heat was getting oppressive, and she removed as much of her clothing as presentable and stripped the children of their undershirts, jackets and stocking. Other passengers had done the same, sacrificing extra clothing for a slight relief from heat.

The train to Glencoe was modest compared to "The Orange Blossom Special." Its seats were harder and closer together. It chugged along much slower and stopped often in small towns, smaller than one block in her old Brooklyn neighborhood.

Leah had never seen a population that had as many black people as white. She was puzzled about their relationship and hoped they lived peacefully together. Even in New York City, there were sometimes harsh comments about Jews, but that had never bothered her. She was proud of her people and had always lived in mostly Jewish communities.

With huffs and puffs, the train finally pulled into Glencoe. Mose was standing by the side of the rails with a big smile and bouquet of flowers. When she stepped off the train car, he gathered them all in his arms.

Leah protested. "Don't squish the bouquet! So sweet of you but must have cost a lot."

Mose grinned. "You have always loved flowers so you will be most happy here. These were free for the picking in the yard of a customer." This would be the first of many surprises.

The small depot was in the center of town but no taxis were around. An elderly black man came up with a home-made wagon. "Mr. Rosenberg," he said. "I can take yore cases to the store. Y'all go on, and I'll get them off the train and bring them to ya."

Surprise number two. Walking to the store and trusting all their belongings to a stranger. The slow, soft speech of the southern black man had also been pleasant to hear.

She was even more enchanted as they walked the short distance to the store to hear the same rhythm and softness in the speech of the white people also. "Evenin' Mr. Rosenberg, glad to see yore better half and young'uns got here."

"Howdy do, Mam."

"Let me know if I can hep ya get settled in."

Not only do they sound different, thought Leah, *but the words are not what we would say. It is afternoon—not evening. Young'uns must mean children—but what is Mose's "better half"? I expected that our language would be the same.* Surprise three.

Mose said, "Close your eyes," and led her the remaining short half-block to the store.

She had expected a small shop squeezed among other shops on a crowded street. Instead, she saw an imposing brick edifice with a broad show window on each side of the door. In large gold printed letters on both sides was simply "Rosenberg's Department Store." One window attractively displayed a few pieces of ladies' apparel and the other clothes for gentlemen.

"Mose, darling, how did you acquire this beautiful store and the merchandise? I can't believe what I am seeing."

"It wasn't like this when I came. I cleaned, painted, and scrubbed floors and counters until I found the real beauty of the place. It had sat vacant since the owner gave up and went back north—but that won't happen to Rosenberg's."

"No, it will not. We will both work hard to make our

business prosper and to establish a home here." She stopped and looked around. "I can't imagine where you found money for merchandise like this."

"Well, I haven't told you before, but we have a partner, The Bank of Glencoe. They were eager to have a store selling fashionable, good-quality merchandise in the town. Seems their wives had been riding the train to Savannah to buy special outfits. The bank president, Mr. Dolby, didn't want that money leaving town. He wanted all the shopping done here in Glencoe. He financed me and will be part owner until the loan is paid off."

"How did you get knowledge of all of this when you have never been here or met the man?" This surprise was enormous enough to count as number four and five.

Mose led them inside and proudly gave his family a tour. Leah was quiet and trying to reconcile all of this in her mind.

My father made his living from a push cart in the garment district—now we own a store fit for Manhattan. Well, not quite that fancy, but certainly better than I could have dreamed.

"The former owner turned out to be one of my mother's distant cousins. He put it up for sale in our community newspaper. I answered it, and he put me in touch with Mr. Dolby." Surprises six and seven.

If anyone can do this, it would be my husband. He has worked in retail stores since he was a boy.

"But Mose, does this mean that if we fail, the store will belong to Mr. Dolby?"

"We will not fail, Leah. Our grandchildren will own this store."

Leah looked in her husband's eyes and had no more doubts.

"Absolutely, we will not fail, and we will dress all the ladies and gentlemen of Glencoe in finery from Rosenberg's."

Before making the decision to make their home in the south, Mose and Leah discussed the differences they would incur. Isolation from their Jewish culture would be difficult. Few, if any Jews, would be living near them. A place to worship was not nearby. It would be difficult to observe their traditions and customs.

Leah interpreted this to mean that some Jews were in Glencoe but fewer than Brooklyn. She learned differently on her first day after the move when she set out to shop for food for their first Sabbath.

Mose had explained that it was necessary for the store to be open on Saturday, since that was the only day when farmers came to town to shop. He would work on Saturday, but he did not expect Leah to do so.

Together, they decided to adjust and observe the Sabbath as best they could. They would set aside Friday evening and follow all the traditions of their faith. He staunchly promised to close one Saturday each month and take the family to a temple in Savannah.

Mose knew that transportation would be the problem. It would take two hours to get to Savannah and it would be costly—but he believed he owed it to Leah. She has already sacrificed so much. Mose would make the plan work.

He advertised for a driver and a young man came forward who was happy to be paid to drive to Savannah and enjoy the city for a few hours once a month.

The promise to close one Saturday each month was kept

until Mose was able to hire an assistant who could manage the store on Saturday. The Saturdays the store closed were referred to in Glencoe as Jewish Holidays.

Leah took her shopping basket and began her first visits to the stores on Glencoe's Main Street. She planned an elaborate meal for their Friday night Sabbath dinner. Her candle arbors and other dishes were polished and a small table set. A nice brisket, fresh Challah bread and boiled potatoes would be perfect—and a sweet cake for the children.

Finding no bakery was her first disappointment. When she inquired at the grocer about buying bread, he told that he didn't stock loafbread because folks in Glencoe made cornbread and biscuits. She absorbed this information and thought for a moment. *I will just have to keep yeast and make my own bread. Actually, I will enjoy baking as my mother always baked fresh bread each day.*

When she asked to see a brisket at the grocers, he replied, "Ma'am, that's beef, ain't it? We don't carry beef except when some of the farmers need cash and kill a heifer to sell. "

She had to stifle a gag at that horrible thought, but she knew that was true of all meats. She had never thought of how it got into the butcher shop.

The only meat available was pork, which, by tradition, they did not eat. A few small chickens with no fat on their bodies completed the meat selections.

For the first time since she'd arrived, tears of loneliness filled her eyes. The grocer had never seen a customer cry over meat before, and the tears were more than he could take. "Mrs.

Rosenberg, I know you are used to a lot more than I have to offer, but I think I do have something you might enjoy. How would you like a nice fat hen?"

"Oh, that would be lovely," she said. I can make a hearty soup and also serve baked chicken. I will take that."

"Come in the back with me and pick out the one you want. I have several."

Leah followed him through a curtain and was astonished to see a pen of hens strutting around, scratching for food and cackling. She had not expected this, and almost said no, but she steeled herself and accepted yet another part of her new life.

"Give me the fattest one of the lot. I need chicken fat for my soup." She didn't bother to ask if it would be kosher. Her mother had kept a strict kosher kitchen, but Leah's life was different now.

"You picked a good one. I will get her picked and cleaned and delivered to you. Next time I get in a slab of beef, I will save a piece for ya."

He didn't ask her address—everyone in Glencoe knew where everyone lived. The one item on her list that the store offered was potatoes, but they were not like potatoes she had ever seen. The grocer assured her that the small, round, red potatoes were the same as the long brown ones she had known.

"One other thing I need is candles."

The grocer shook his head. "Ma'am, I don't carry those, but James MacTavish across the street has a store full of such stuff."

Despite all of the new surprises, their first southern Sabbath dinner was perfect.

Mose's prediction of the store's success came true, and instead of customers going out of town to shop, the reverse happened. Shoppers from out of town started coming to Glencoe to buy the latest fashions at Rosenberg's. Both Leah and Mose, it seemed, had an eye for style and good business sense.

They acquired a house after the first year, but Leah continued to keep the back room partially furnished as a place to keep the children and prepare quick meals. Mose installed a bell on the front door so they could hear when people came in from the back room. Both enjoyed the traffic of customers and some who just came in to visit. They made friends with the townspeople, and the townspeople became their friends.

During the second year of the store's opening, Leah was in the backroom serving lunch to her children when the bell tinkled. She hurried to the front and saw the most beautiful young girl she had seen in Glencoe standing meekly by the counter. "Welcome to Rosenberg's, my dear. May I be of service to you?" At first, Leah thought she might have been Jewish because of her coloring, but when she spoke there was no mistaking that she was not.

The voice was so soft and low that Leah had to strain to hear. "Yessum, I'm gettin' me a dress made by Miz Steptoe and need to buy material. She wrote down what I need to make a dress and a petticoat." She avoided looking into Leah's eyes.

Leah took the slip of paper and walked right to a bolt of white voile with tiny patterns of yellow flowers worked into the material. "This would be lovely for you. How do you like it?"

"Oh ma'am, that's the prettiest material I ever seen. What else do I need?"

Leah measured off the correct yardage and added buttons, lace and soft muslin for the petticoat. "My, my this is beginning to look like a wedding dress to me."

The girl looked right into Leah's eyes for the first time and a sly smile covered her face. "Yessum, it's to be my weddin' dress."

The girl looked not more than fifteen, but everything about her seemed mature and ready for marriage.

Leah reached under the counter and brought out a lace handkerchief. "Since this is a wedding dress, I have a gift for you."

"I shore thank ya, Ma'am. I ain't never seen such a pretty handkerchief."

"I want to give you this to wish you happiness, good fortune and many children. Now tell me the name of this fortunate young man."

"His name's James MacTavish."

"James MacTavish! My, my, he is quite a dashing young man. I know you will be very happy."

The cost of the material and notions was $4.30—the most money Myra, the young lady, had ever spent. As she closed the door, she thought of the lady inside. *She shore wuz a fine lady and helped me a lot. I hadn't ever knowed a Jew before, but if they all as nice as Miz Rosenberg, they are mighty good folks.*

The young bride became one of the town's most beloved and respected citizens.

Leah and Myra had a lifelong bond of friendship, but their

visits together only occurred in the store. They greeted each other only as "Mrs. Rosenberg" and "Mrs. MacTavish." Both had thoughts of the pleasure of sitting on a porch, chatting and watching their children play together, but neither knew how to initiate this step.

In the years that followed, both Rosenberg children acquired Southern accents. Leah had grown to love the Southern people, but she did have concern about her children's lack of exposure to their Hebrew heritage and sent them to a month-long Hebrew camp in the Catskills each summer.

Neither of Mose and Leah's children showed interest in the store or expressed any desire to inherit it. This disappointed Mose, but Leah pointed out how much wider their world would be when they were adults. He agreed and proudly allowed them to make their own life choices. Both chose to attend college in the north.

As the Great Depression waned to an end, news from Europe destroyed any hope of peace in the world. The horrors happening to Jews in Europe touched the hearts of even this small town in south Georgia. Every day the newspapers were filled with the atrocities of Adolph Hitler and his Nazi followers.

The Rosenbergs' New York relatives sent clippings from the more extensive coverage in their newspapers. The inhumanity was unbelievable—but starkly true.

Both sides of their families were second generation immigrants from Poland. Many of their family members were caught in what would come to be called the Holocaust.

They were helpless to give aid or hope to their beloved family members still in Poland. Until a letter arrived, that is.

Dear Mose and Leah,

We are so blessed to be safe and secure in the United States, but that is not true of all of our family. I have had correspondence through a source in Switzerland with our cousin, Saul, in Warsaw.

The terror and distress that we read in the newspapers is happening to their neighbors, friends, and family. No Jew is safe in Poland. Trains are filled daily with Jews to be sent to the prison camps. Like the rest of our family, we know you have them in your heart and want to help.

Saul's grandson, Ruben, is eighteen years old. He was able to secure passage for the boy to get out of Poland and enter Holland. From Holland, he boarded a merchant ship that will dock in Savannah, Georgia within the next few weeks. It will be dangerous, and possibly not successful, but what he has to face if he does not take this chance is unthinkable.

Since he will be landing near you, we ask you to give the boy a home. He is a fine lad, I am told—very smart, mannerly, and also lucky if his voyage is successful. I know this is short notice, but I just received the information. Please give this boy a chance.

With my love,

Your brother Abe

Mose read the letter aloud and then handed to Leah. She read silently and then looked at her husband. "Can we do this? He is a stranger to us."

Mose pulled his spectacles down on his nose, wiped his eyes, and studied his wife's face. "Can we *not* do this? We are strangers to *him*. He is leaving everything behind. We have everything."

A friend from the temple in Savannah where they worshiped was employed by a shipping company. Mose contacted him to ask about the schedule of ships coming into Savannah. Few ships arrived in Savannah from Holland, so it was easy to learn when the boy would arrive.

Two weeks later Mose and Isaac drove to Savannah to picked up their Polish cousin, Ruben. The boy was everything his brother had described. He learned English easily and became a great asset to the store. It was also such a delight to have the family sit together at the Sabbath meal and speak Hebrew. He seemed to be adjusting to life in the United States, but often they heard the boy weeping in the night. Leah and Mose left him to his private grief, but they often wept for him.

Rosenberg's continued to prosper as a hallmark destination for south Georgia shoppers. Mose's dream was that his son would carry on the family institution. That was not to be.

Before the United States went to war, Isaac spent two years studying in college. He wanted to be a doctor, but as he learned more about the atrocities done to his people, he could not wait to get into the fight. He went to Canada and became a flyer with the British RAF. Word spread that he was an ace and always hit his targets on missions over Germany.

After many missions, Mose and Leah received a telegram from President Roosevelt. Their precious boy had gone down in flames. Later a letter from a crew member told them, "Issac had dropped his load of bombs and was headed back to base."

Rachel followed her brother's ambition. She became a doctor and married one, too. After she finished Columbia Medical School and the war had ended, she and her husband came to Glencoe for a visit, and they announced their future plans.

"Jews now have their own nation, and we want to be a part of it. Herman and I are moving to Israel and will become citizens. We must do our part to make a great Jewish State." Though sad to see them go, Mose and Leah were proud of their daughter.

Mose neared retirement, and with both of their children gone, there was no heir to inherit Rosenberg's. He lamented this to Leah, and she laughed out loud.

"Don't be silly, Mose. He is sitting right under your nose."

Ruben had learned every facet of the business from his cousin—and Rosenberg's Department Store continued on Main Street Glencoe, Georgia for several generations.

The Country Bride

In the deepest of the Great Depression, a wedding that was a bride's dream come true was given for Laura James and Carlton by her family. From her savings as a dental assistant, Laura James had been able to buy a special dress. Aunt Molly presented her a bouquet of flowers to hold when she stood beside her groom. Carlton wore a suit and tie, a fresh haircut and a grin that wouldn't stop. His pride and adoration when he looked at his bride brought happy tears to the eyes of her mama and papa.

The family had been through hard times, but this day was a celebration. Having their home and almost everything they owned burn to the ground in the midst of the greatest depression ever experienced in the country brought times when it had been a struggle to fill the bellies of their family. Their oldest daughter had added to their grief when she had run off and married a man older than her papa.

It had gotten so bad that Myra struggled even to pray. There was so much need. Then, like a tree budding out in the earliest days of spring—here came Carlton with his sparkling blue eyes and a smile from ear to ear.

The lives of the MacTavishes seemed to turn a good corner from that day forward. Carlton worshipped the ground where their Laura James walked. He was only a poor boy from a neighboring county, but he had a dream and the determination to make it come true. James was happy to shake the hand of this young fellow and announce to all of the MacTavish gathered for the wedding, "I am proud of this marriage."

After the wedding dinner, bountiful but mostly homemade gifts, and all the congratulations and good wishes, it was time for Laura James to leave and go with her new husband to a place she had never seen. She was happy to climb into the Model-A Ford loaned to them by Carlton's father, and start life with a man who planned to earn their living from pine trees.

Carlton cranked the sputtering engine, and they headed down the highway. As soon as they were out of sight of the family, he pulled the car into a little lane and gave his bride the big kiss he was too bashful to do in front of her family. Now she was his wife, and he would be with her every day for the rest of his life.

The forty miles from Glencoe, the only home she had ever known, to the farm near Norristown passed quickly. The Model-A had been cleaned and shined to a mirror finish, tuned up, tires filled and every detail covered to give his bride a smooth ride. Their only conversation was about the wedding and how nice the family had treated them. He knew Laura James was nervous about meeting his pa and settling into a new setting. The grin stayed plastered to his face, and Laura

James wore her small sweet smile all through the ride.

As they approached what looked like a town in the distance, Carlton looked at his bride. "Okay, honey, we're coming up on Norristown. It ain't much of a town after you've been used to Glencoe, but it's a right nice little place."

"Oh, Carlton, look at all the people gathered around the stores. It is a bigger place than you made out."

That pleased him beyond measure because he had feared she would look down on such a small village. "It's Saturday, and that is when most everyone around here comes into town. There's two nice stores, a post office, a bank and our church. Dang, I forgot to point out the church to ya when we passed."

Laura James smiled at her brand new husband. "Do you know what Norristown looks like to me?"

"Nope, I shore don't."

"Well, to me, it looks like home."

Hearing that filled his heart with a pride in his wife that he would never lose. He would have stopped for another kiss and hug, but they were turning off the highway onto the lane leading to his papa's land.

The one-lane bumpy road made a zig-zagged path through the thick growth of pine trees on both sides. Laura James felt smothered by the trees, but she did not comment.

"This is where our livin' is comin' from Laura James. I've worked chipping boxes ever since I come back home, and I'm nearly finished."

"What does that mean?" She was pictured him chopping up boxes and couldn't see any value in that.

"I cut a slash in the tree and put a tin bucket under it to catch the tar that starts to flowing out of it in the spring. That's what I went to Glencoe to learn how to do. Stephen taught me all about it."

She was totally confused. "How does that make money?"

"When it starts filling the buckets, we go through the woods and dip it out of the bucket into barrels that we take to the still. They pay us for every barrel we take."

"What does the still do with it?"

"Tell the truth, I don't know how it's done, but the tar turns into something called turpentine and that's used for all kinda things. Remember, that's what Stephen's wife's pa came to Glencoe to teach the Meadows."

"Tomorrow you can walk the woods with me and see how the chippins done. I'd thought Stephen had told you all about it."

She still did not understand, but she liked the idea of walking through the woods with Carlton. Just then, the car hit a big bump that nearly knocked them through the roof of the car.

"Dang gummit," said Carlton, "I was so into talkin' that I forgot to slow down for the cattle guard. " He stopped the car and got out to see if he had done any damage. Laura James followed him.

Carlton inspected the front of the Model-A and sighed. "It looks like I didn't hurt nothin'. I'd shore hate to tell Pa if I tore up his car. See the cattle guard there." Four aged and stripped logs were embedded in the road with a space between each. Strange looking thing to be in the road, and someone must have put it there.

As if reading Laura James' thoughts, he said, "That's to keep the cows from gettin' off our land. The spaces keep them from walking cross 'cause they scared've fallin' through. Cows are smart like that."

This gave her a good laugh to think of the cows being scared of falling through the spaces. She did have a lot to learn about living in this wild country. Her only comment was, "I will remind you of that cattle guard the next time we go this way. I shore don't want to hit the car roof again."

Around the next curve, they reached a little log house and in front of it stood all of Carlton's family—his papa, stepma, two brothers, little sister, baby brother and an older sister. They all hung back and stared at Laura James. Mr. Lee stepped forward and extended his hand to her. "We're proud to have you here with us. I hope you can be happy living in these woods."

"Thank you, Mr. Lee. I will be happy anywhere if I am with Carlton. I might be from town, but my mama taught me to work like country folks."

Carlton made her acquainted with each one of them. No one said anything except his sister, Margaret, who said, "Jewel told me all about meetin' you in Glencoe. She shore thinks a lot of ya. I live a few miles off with my husband, Harmon, but close enough that we can get to be friends."

Mr. Lee interrupted. "Little lady, I believe you'll be a help to all of us. Now y'all let me show ya how I fixed up the log house for ya. It's old but it's still sturdy. My grandpa built it for my ma and pa to live in when they first wed." Mr. Lee led them across the road and opened the door to the log house.

Laura James was a little nervous to see this strange new home, but when she stepped inside, she was delighted. One big room was the length of the cabin, and a little kitchen was built onto the side. The first thing she noticed was a big stone fireplace that almost covered the end wall. It was already filled with logs waiting to be lit to take the chill off the early spring air. The wide pine boards of the floor had been cleaned and smoothed to a soft shine. A long table with benches and two rocking chairs filled the front space, and in the rear, was an iron bed covered with a quilt and a small table holding a big oil lamp. The kitchen held only a wood stove and shelves across the wall for storing things. The cabin was cozy and just the right place to start her life with Carlton.

"Little lady, you need to look here at what's on the shelves." Her eyes went immediately to a set of three green pottery bowls, and she could not help squealing her glee.

That made Mr. Lee chuckle. "I bought them bowls from a man parked in a wagon beside the road. He made 'em from clay down by the river. I don't know how he got them so hard and painted green, but he musta known how. When I saw 'em I said to myself, 'That's just the right thing to help Carlton and his gal set up housekeeping.'"

Laura James wanted to hug and thank him, but she knew that wasn't his way. She smiled big, and said, "I am so proud to have these pretty bowls. Thank ya for givin' me just what I need."

"You're shore welcome. We got some housekeeping stuff in the barn that we ain't usin'. Some of it's been there since I broke up my ma's house when she died. You welcome to whatever you can use."

"Thank you again, Mr. Lee." She already knew that she had a good friend in him. "I'll come up there tomorrow and help myself."

Sadie, *his* new wife, had not said a word. She continued to look Laura James up and down with a scowl on her face. That made the new bride a little concerned for her welcome. Carlton had told her that his pa's new wife was hard to get to know and suspicious of everyone.

Just before leaving, Sadie said in a rough voice, "There ain't no stores close by except them in Norristown. You can't be running back and forth there, and you'd spend a lotta money. We got a smokehouse full of meat, more eggs that we can eat. The cows give rich milk, and I make butter nearly every day. They be plenty of vegetables soon, and 'till then, I got plenty of jars filled. Come up to the house and hep yoreself. Be shore and get a jug of syrup 'cause Carlton loves that better than anything— exceptin' maybe you. I be cookin' supper soon, so y'all come on up and eat with us, but don't plan to make a habit of it."

Everyone laughed except Sadie, and Laura James knew, in spite of all, she had another friend. Remembering the scarcities her family had known during the Depression, she wished she could share this bounty with them.

After the family headed home, Laura James saw a little face looking at her around the corner of the house.

Carlton bent over and peered at the little face himself. "What you doin' hiding back there, Patsy?"

No answer, and the little face ducked out of sight. Laura James pretended to go inside, but sneaked around to the back of the house. "Gotcha," she said as she put her arms around Carlton's little sister and pulled her close. Still no answer. The little girl squirmed and tried to get out of the arms locked around her.

Laura James was persistent. "You ain't goin' nowhere, Miss Patsy. I need you to come in and help me put my things away." The little girl was light as a feather, so Laura James picked her up and carried her to the porch swing where Carlton was sitting.

"Whatcha got there?" he said.

"Something I picked up in the backyard, but she ain't gettin' away until she helps me put my things away."

"By tomorrow you'll have stopped sayin' Patsy cause she's a Skeeter and will bother you to death."

Skeeter started giggling, and Laura James had another friend. From that day on, Carlton's little sister spent most of her days following Laura James' every step. She had never known her mother and devoured any affection. She also filled a spot in Laura James' heart that ached from homesickness for her own family.

On the second morning, two little faces appeared at the cabin door—little brother, Petie, who came for the day and continued arriving every morning. There was a family of four at most every meal.

Mr. Lee's farm was the land of plenty, and he generously shared with his son and new daughter-in-law. Aside from the homegrown foods, he kept a big flour barrel filled and sacks of sugar. He even bought coffee beans to grind. Every meal was a feast. Laura James ate so many eggs that she thought she might start cackling.

Carlton went to the woods right after daylight so the children were company. She made them coffee milk with lots of sugar to join in her second cup of coffee. They usually sat in the swing, wrapped together in a quilt for warmth while she told them all of the stories she remembered from her childhood or taught them songs from her Sunday School days. There was a lot of cuddling going on, and the two children adored this time.

Patsy had always dressed in overalls like her brothers. Mr. Lee kept her hair cut short since he did not know how to do otherwise. Laura James first challenge was to make Skeeter into a little girl before she started to school.

She discussed this with her father-in-law, and he agreed to turn the hair trims over to her. Dresses came next. She had found a workable sewing machine that had belonged to Carlton's mother and was now stored in the barn. Her mother Myra's sewing skills had passed on to her, and she had also learned sewing in home economics in school.

"Mr. Lee, you said I could have whatever I needed from the stuff stored in the old barn. If you will let me use that sewing machine, I can make some school dresses for Patsy before she starts next fall."

He broke into a grin from ear to ear. "I want her to have some pretty dresses. If her ma had lived, she would be sewing up a storm making dresses for her. Ole Skeeter's right pretty now that you're trimmin' her hair like you do. Next week when

I go to the stockyard, you can go along and buy what you need. I can pay for whatever you want to get."

"That will be wonderful. Could we take her and Petie with us? It will be good for them to get away from the place for a while." She knew that neither of them had even been the ten miles to Swainsboro.

"Shore, and I wanna buy Skeeter some shoes like girls' wear. Can you handle both of 'em while I'm at the stock yard most of the day? There's a hamburger place there that y'all can eat."

This fit Laura James' plans perfectly. Her sister, Idella, lived in Swainsboro, so maybe she could also visit and see her little niece.

Carlton's prediction of making a good living from the pine trees was more than fulfilled. The profits his papa shared with him grew into a substantial savings. After Patsy and Petie started to school, Laura James found that she could do all of her housework, cook, and give Carlton any assistances needed and still have time on her hands. Like her mama, Myra, she did not know how to be idle, so she found employment at a woolen mill in a nearby town. In no time, she had shown her value to the company and was continually given promotions.

Although she had to get up and leave home before daylight, she enjoyed the work and also the increasing pay checks she received. They continued to live modestly, and soon the savings from her salary and his earnings enabled them to buy a large track of land covered with pines.

Years before, Mr. Lee had given his oldest son the old home place where his grandparents had lived. Little by little, Carlton repaired and renovated the home into a country showplace. The house was large enough for the children they were hoping to add to their family.

The pine trees grew and brought more "turpentine gold" to them each year. Laura James became a supervisor of an area of the mill. They moved into the renovated house which offered every convenience known at that time. They were waiting for their children to fill up the rooms set aside for them…but no children came.

After seeing the growing families of their brothers and sisters, they lost hope of ever being parents. Their last resort was to take their dilemma to a specialist in Augusta and ask for help.

"Mr. and Mrs. Larson, I cannot find any physical reason that you cannot conceive and bear children.'

"It ain't that we've not been trying." Immediately Carlton was embarrassed at what had slipped out of his mouth.

The doctor laughed and tried to put them at ease. "This is one of the things in life that we do not understand yet. Hopefully, we will have more knowledge later, but for now let's look at your problem."

Laura was holding back tears. "Doctor, I just feel like we have so much love and a good home for a child. I pray about it all the time, and it seems like God would want us to have a child."

"My dear, you and Carlton should have a child or many children. I have never met any couple who had more to offer to a child. I would suggest adoption to you, but that is a long process, and sometimes it is discouraging."

"I've thought of that, doctor, but I felt like Carlton would want his own flesh and blood children."

Carlton's head swung around. "Now you stop right there, Miss Laura James. What in the hell gave you that idea? They will be our own no matter where they come from. Tell us more, doctor. You sound pretty discouraging about adoption."

"Carlton, there are many, many little children out there needing a home. Many of them are not eligible to be adopted for one reason or another. Foster parents are needed badly to care for them. "

"What do you mean *foster* parents?" Both almost spoke at once.

"These are children who for one reason or another cannot be legally adopted, and they live in the foster care system until they come of age."

"You mean we could get one and might have to give it back?" Laura James knew she could not take this heartbreak.

"They would stay with you as long as they need you. Sometimes they can return to their family, and that is good. Until they have a chance for a good home, they will remain with you."

Laura James still did not think she could stand having a child leave her after she had grown to love it like her own.

Carlton broke in. "Honey, it would not be different than if we had our own young'uns. They all grow up and leave. That's just the natural way. That don't mean they stop lovin' ya. I think what the Lord means for us to do is to provide for and love one of these little throw-aways. Doctor, we'll take whatever you've got." He looked over at his wife. She was smiling and nodding yes.

The doctor smiled, too. "You have made a good decision. Some little children will be mighty blessed to have you as their parents. Now, it won't happen overnight, but I will start the process."

In a few weeks, a little seven-year-old boy with red hair and freckles named Benny became their foster son. He trailed behind Carlton's every step and Laura Jean kept the cookie jar filled. Since they had met their goal of owning land, Laura James was ready to be a stay-at-home mother.

In the coming years, all the rooms in their house were filled with foster children. Their long dining table was always loaded with food and over the years, it served more than a dozen hungry appetites. Some stayed throughout their school years, and some left early when circumstances allowed a return to their family. Carlton and Laura James were sad to see them leave, but also happy to have provided for them and loved them when the children needed it most.

In their later years, all of the children kept in touch and often visited. Age caught up with the young couple, and Carlton's hard-working days in the woods were over. He did not want to sell the land he cherished, but how could he keep it up?

The answer came one Christmas Day when their holiday table was filled by Benny and his family.

"Pa, I have never wanted to do anything in my life except work in the woods like you taught me. I'm doing right well in the mill in South Carolina, but we want our young'uns to be raised in the place where I was raised. How about we move back here so I can help you?"

Having a child must not have been God's plan for Carlton and Laura James. He needed them to love and care for far more than one.

Mr. Porter

Mr. Jacobson warmly shook the hand of LeGrand Porter. "I welcome your help. I must sell at least half of my merchandise to get enough cash to keep the store open. Thank you for coming this week to get us started for the big sale next week."

"I'm glad to be able to help, Marvin," said LeGrant. "During this depression, even the best merchants like you are facing tough times. Our first job is finding incentives to bring customers into the store."

LeGrand was from Swainsboro and had earned a reputation as a promoter who could run a successful sale and attract customers. His personality, showmanship and tactics had succeeded in several nearby towns and brought curious customers into the stores. Even in the hardest of times, folks were enticed to part with a little of their money to purchase an item that would bring some joy to their lives.

"It's in your hands now, LeGrand, and I will do whatever you say." Mr. Jacobson, the store owner was relieved to hand his worries over to someone with a reputation of turning failing businesses around. Unpaid bills were making the fear of bankruptcy a real threat.

"We've got a full week to get ready and make folks wonder what is going on at Jacobson's. We'll put signs everywhere we can stick them to tell about all the savings and free gifts for all who come into the store. They won't come in intending to buy—but their eyes will take in the sale merchandise." LeGrand had seen this succeed before and knew his first effort was always to convince the store owner that promotions would pay off in the end."

"How can I give out free gifts when I'm nearly bankrupt? What kind of gifts?" This was the response LeGrand expected and was prepared to answer.

"A folding paper fan for all the ladies. Cheap, because I buy in bulk and have plenty in my car. I guarantee that every lady in Glencoe will have a fan by the end of next week. The ladies will not resist the chance to get something colorful and different."

Mr. Jacobson rubbed his hands nervously. "Nothing is cheap for me when I hardly have two quarters to rub together. I can't go along with them coming in just for something free and then walking right out."

LeGrand stared around the store before saying more. "Well, if that is your decision, I'll head back to Swainsboro."

"No, no, I want you to put on the sale. Just tell me how that is going to help."

"Well, Mr. Jacobson, first we will hang a big banner in front with paintings of fans and invite all the ladies to come in for a free gift. Signs all around town will announce BIG SALE ALL

PRICES REDUCED. The words "cheap" and "bargain" will be used on every sign. Next, we will rearrange the store, pile goods up on tables to look like there might be something wrong with those items—that makes folks feel they are getting a bargain. And they will be, because everything will be reduced at least ten percent."

"With you getting ten percent of all the sales and another ten percent lost on the merchandise, I will be in worse shape than I am now."

LeGrand gave a big chuckle before saying, "How much is your regular markup?"

Very sheepishly, Mr. Jacobson said, "We'll go your way. I hope you're not planning on making a profit selling me those fans." LeGrand did not give an answer and knew the store owner was ready to give him a free hand with the sale, so he added more.

"A few other things. We will give every child a sucker and every man a chance ticket for a drawing to get a shoat pig on the last day of the sale."

"Since you are bringing in extra sales help, I'd like a young lady assigned to help me throughout the next two weeks."

Mr. Jacobson grinned. "I expected that and hired two ladies last week for temporary work during the sale. They will be coming in tomorrow. One is experienced and worked for over twenty years in one of our local stores that went bankrupt. The other is a young woman with no experience but from her family background, I expect her to have a real knack for selling. You can decide who you would like to be your helper."

The next morning Idella MacTavish and the other saleslady were waiting at the door when Mr. Jacobson arrived to open. Idella was eager to begin her first job, especially since she and her family were suffering all the hardships of the depression. *Now, maybe I can earn enough during these two weeks to at least buy some of the personal things I have had to do without for so long. If I'm good at sales, maybe this will turn into a full-time job. Wouldn't Papa be surprised? It'll serve him right for the way he has been showing his tail, drinking and running around.*

Just as they walked into the store, a man who was a stranger to Idella parked a shiny black Packard in front and entered as if he were an employee or even an owner. "Mrs. Strange and Miss MacTavish, meet Mr. Porter. He is from Swainsboro and will be in charge of the sale. You are to do whatever he asks of you." Both women nodded.

Mr. Porter first asked the ladies to start sorting the merchandise according to price. Mrs. Strange knew the stock well and did not need his direction. That was good, but he could not take his eyes from the younger woman, who seemed uneasy and hesitant. Soon his gaze was not to judge her workmanship but just for the pure pleasure of viewing her beauty. He knew she was way too young for him to be having these thoughts, but he could not deny himself the chance to be near her.

"Mrs. Strange, you know the value of our merchandise and how it should be displayed on the tables. Will you take the responsibility of preparing the sale tables?" The older lady was flattered to be given this responsibility.

He turned to Idella. "Miss MacTavish, will you be my

assistant in preparing all of the promotions?" Idella could not have been happier. She did not want to spend the next two weeks sorting through socks and underwear. Mr. Porter could teach her a lot. Any man driving a new Packard in these hard times must know things other folks did not.

LeGrand kept her near him on the first day. *She is so lovely and also intelligent. I wonder how old she is.*

Idella had thoughts also. *He is such a gentleman, well dressed and must be highly educated. I wonder how old he is…and if he's married."*

By noon they had become LeGrand and Idella, and he had invited her to have noon dinner with him at the inn where he was staying. A good dinner sounded appealing enough—she wanted to find out more about this mystery man. As they walked up the sidewalk, she found enough nerve to ask, "Is your wife here with you or does she stay at home with the children?"

He did not hesitate to tell her that his wife had passed away five years before and that his children were grown and no longer lived at home. She tried to calculate how old that would make him but stopped those thoughts. Age was unimportant with a mannerly, well-groomed businessman who owned a Packard.

The filling noon dinners at the Sunny Inn continued through the week. She enjoyed having meat and satisfying her hunger instead of making do with the scant meals her mama had to prepare. She enjoyed the excitement at the way this mature and successful man made her feel like she was someone special.

The sale began on Monday, and a line snaked down the street before the door opened. Idella stood near the door and gave out the fans and suckers.

From their excitement, you would have thought the folks were receiving gold. The newly-weaned shoat pig was shown off in a pen by the side of the store. Men gathered around for a look and each declared that he would be the winner. The pen stunk to high heaven but that didn't seem to matter.

Idella laughed when she thought of how much her mama would value that pig if her papa won it. Of course, James MacTavish wouldn't come near the store and see his daughter working when he could not find a job.

During the week of the sale, LeGrand was too busy to go out for dinner at noon. Everyone either brought lunch or made do with a Coke and cheese crackers.

Both missed each other's company. On the first day of the sale, LeGrand suggested that they have supper together after the store closed, and told her that he would drive her home.

The first night when she returned later than usual, riding in Legrand's Packard, all hell broke loose. Mama said terrible things about why an old man like him would waste time and money on a foolish young girl. Papa forbade her to be with LeGrand except during the working day.

That did not stop their suppers together or the rides home. Her papa's and mama's only hope was that at the end of the week of the sale, Le Grand Porter would return to Swainsboro.

It did not work out that way. When the sale ended Idella was hired as a full-time employee of Jacobson's, and LeGrand continued to come every Sunday and take her to dinner at the Sunny Inn.

Myra had tired of hearing enough about the "best fried chicken Idella had ever eaten," and James was suspicious of why Mr. Jacobson would hire a young inexperienced girl to work full time when so many well-experienced and respected salesclerks were unemployed. He threatened to turn his gun on LeGrand if the affair continued. On top of all the hardships the family was enduring, this was tearing them apart.

A new young man, Autry, appeared and started taking Idella to the picture show. James even eavesdropped by the window one night and heard then "sparking" on the porch. This was a good sign that his daughter had come to her senses. She seemed happy with Autry, and her parents rejoiced that the LeGrand crisis had passed.

Meanwhile, Idella and LeGrand had been using the store telephone to make other plans. And, after dinner on Christmas Day, Idella announced that this would be her last Christmas with the family. LeGrand would arrive soon to get her, and he had arranged for them to be married that afternoon.

Idella had been secretly moving her belongings to Jacobson's along with a new dress she had bought for the wedding. The time she had spent with Autry was just a distraction. Neither Myra, James, nor her sister Laura James had had a clue of her plans.

LeGrand had her belongings packed in his car when he arrived. When the big Packard pulled up, James went out and tried to shame him about what he was doing to a girl who was young enough to be his daughter. LeGrand's response was, "You are way out of line, Mr. MacTavish. I love her and will do everything I can to make her happy."

Idella hopped in the car and the Packard headed down the road. There was nothing more that could be said or done. The family stood in the road and with broken hearts watched the car until it was out of sight. The next few weeks were like a death, but no one brought flowers or food. Time eased the heartache somewhat, but the breach between Idella and her family was forever strained.

LeGrand never grew comfortable visiting the rambunctious, fun-loving MacTavish family and their visits were usually short. It upset Idella that her husband did not stay in the company of the family but usually found a quiet place to read or listen to the radio. Idella felt torn between her family and husband.

"You ignore my husband," she accused her family and to her husband, she ranted, "You can't get to know my family when all you do is keep your nose stuck in a book while we are with them." Visits were especially stressful for Myra who wanted the family to be close and enjoy their times together.

Idella's marriage helped her escape the hardships of the Great Depression but it added a new pain—loneliness. During the first years of marriage, they lived in the family home with LeGrand's mother. She was kind and understanding with her young daughter-in-law, but she inwardly had concerns about the adjustments that both Idella and LeGrand must make since they were so far apart in age and their needs seemed to be so conflicting.

The Porters lived on a prominent street of homes, but all the neighbors were near the age of the senior Mrs. Porter. A maid did all the household chores and cooking.

Idella had no duties—not even the care of her own clothes. Days were spent visiting on the front porch with neighbors who dropped by. Their conversations were about health, illness, or people that Idella did not know and things that happened before she was born. She always felt they were judging her critically, especially when she was asked her age.

Spending money was plentiful. LeGrand had accounts in all the stores, and his bride was free to purchase whatever she chose. But she soon tired of shopping. Buying a new dress did not excite her as in the past.

After the excitement of the wedding and a three-day honeymoon in Florida, LeGrand was ready to return to his routine and comforts of home. His work as a sales promoter ended when the Depression lessened, and he was ready to stay home with his mother and wife instead of traveling to a new town every week.

Even though he had never taken the bar exam, he was able to work at a position in the courthouse where he could apply his legal knowledge. Life was satisfying for him. He enjoyed his work, the good meals prepared by Wilma, the families' long-time cook, reading or listening to the radio news, and retiring early to bed with his lovely young wife. He was a lucky man.

That began to change after the first few weeks. Idella frequently suggested going downtown to have a hamburger supper or to see a movie. He encouraged her to make friends with other younger women and do these things during the day. *Goodness knows,* he thought. *She has money to buy or do whatever she pleases.*

This was not a good plan since the younger women did not have money or time to spare and LeGrand's evenings were not as pleasant as he had expected because Idella was often in a bad mood and tended to pout. His mother tried to find ways to interest her in church activities, but she resented this. He had not included thoughts of a child from his marriage with Idella since he had two grown children who had been estranged from him since the death of their mother.

His mother was wise and always tactful, so one evening when Idella had demanded that he take her for a ride and then stormed into the bedroom with a loud slamming of the door when he refused, his mother quietly said, "Son, let's sit on the porch for a bit." They went outside and each took a rocker.

LeGrand shook his head. "Mama, I am so sorry that you have to hear all of this fussing. I know you are not used to your evening being upset, but honest to God, I do not know what to do. I love Idella so dearly and want to make her happy."

"Dear boy, far be it from me to interfere between a wife and husband, but I watch her grow more and more frustrated. She does not have anything in common with my friends or with the younger women either. She has nothing but time on her hands, and the younger women who could be her friends have more to do than they have time because they have young children."

"Mama, you know what a mess I made with my son and

daughter. Both turned their back on me. I am just not up to that again."

"That was not your fault entirely. You were trying to make a living and pay those heavy doctor bills for Eva Gladys. She was sick for so long, and that was hard on you and the children. Both were in their teens, and that was a hard time for them to understand the situation. They had to find someone to blame for losing their mother. Maybe as they grow older, they will understand. You'll be a good father this time. I do believe that a child to love will give Idella fulfillment and keep her busy. I also think you will love being a father again."

The senior Mrs. Porter could not have been more correct. Within a year they had a beautiful, healthy baby girl. She was adored by all, and Idella immediately found new friends when she started rolling little Laura Jean around in her carriage. LeGrand rushed home in the evening for time with his daughter. Visits to the MacTavish grandmother and grandfather became more cordial because everyone wanted time to hold the baby. LeGrand beamed with pride and felt that Mr. MacTavish respected him more since he had become the father of their first grandchild.

Grandmother Porter made full use of her time with the grandchild that she knew would be her last. Laura Jean was a very alert baby from an early age and would sit in her grandmother's lap and listen to Bible stories being read or her grandmother reading letters to her that she had received from missionary friends in China. During the last year of her grandmother's life, two-year-old Laura Jean would tear pages from the Bible Story Book and bring page by page for her grandmother to read.

The home was sold after the death of the older Mrs. Porter, and LeGrand had a new home built that would be near the school and on a street with other children.

Idella was delighted with the move. The new home, their enjoyable neighbors, and their growing daughter gave her the life she had imagined for herself. Then the unexpected happened. A heart attack left Legrand mostly disabled.

With this shadow hanging over her, Idella realized that she must be prepared to raise and support her daughter alone. She made a good decision to take advantage of a government-sponsored business course and learn office skills. She found her calling for the first time, and, upon graduation, started a career. The duties required in running a house and tending a small child had not given her the fulfillment that she craved. A housekeeper took over these duties, and she was able to spend her day in organized work she enjoyed.

Idella loved her husband, but after the heart attack, he had seemed to become an old man. His needs and disposition changed. Their fast-growing, active, curious daughter was often accused of upsetting her father. "Go to your room. Be quiet. Don't bother your father," were the words she most often heard.

LeGrand himself was irritable because of his limitations. Idella let her resentment of his irritability be known. Many harsh words passed between them and Laura Jean became defensive and angry. Home was no longer a happy place.

Legrand died of a massive heart attack when Laura Jean was twelve. After years of being told that she must behave and not cause her father to have another heart attack, the little girl carried an emotional scar for a while. But the love and support of her MacTavish grandparents, aunts and uncles gave her the strength she needed to grow into a gentle and caring adult and find success and love.

In later years, Laura Jean made peace with her mother but followed her own path. She attended the university of her choice by scholarships and part-time jobs. On a Christmas vacation visit, she was surprised when her mother suggested shopping together to pick out a new outfit for her Christmas gift. After she'd outgrown toys, her mother's gift had generally been a card with a check inside. This time mother and daughter actually enjoyed shopping together and picked out a gray and blue plaid skirt and sky-blue sweater.

Walking down the sidewalk to their car, Idella beamed proudly at her grown daughter who would soon be a college graduate, and said, "Laura Jean, I want you to wear your new skirt and sweater to Mama's on Christmas Day. You have become such a pretty young lady. Your eyes are the same blue as your father's and that sweater sets them off perfectly."

The compliment came as more of a surprise than the gift. Since his death, the only mention of Laura Jean's father had been always preceded by: "If only LeGrand had lived and kept his health, we could have or we wouldn't have had to. . ."

Laura tried to picture him in her mind, but all she could bring up was the photograph that hung in her mother's bedroom. It did not show the color of his eyes. This caused her to wonder if maybe she had inherited more of his traits than his blue eyes.

She knew he was studious, enjoyed deep conversations with a few friends, and read continuously. *Huh,* she thought, *sounds familiar.*

"Mama," she said. "Do you think he would be proud of me?"

Idella gazed at her daughter and smiled. "Honey, from the day you were born, he wanted you to soar. And just look at you now."

Mindanao

Where roses do not grow

Chapter I
2000

Neither the backpack under her bottom nor the rolled-up jacket behind her shoulder blades were help in keeping away the weary numbness Laura was feeling in every part of her body. Sitting on a concrete floor with her back against a concrete block wall for three hours had advanced from the level of discomfort to sheer agony. No amount of twisting or squirming gave relief.

Her fanny pack was belted tightly in front of her stomach. Inside was her passport, visa and half of the Philippine currency that Paul had exchanged for their U.S. dollars before leaving San Francisco. She kept clutching it to be sure it was in place. For the time being, the fanny pack was her lifeline.

Twenty hours before, she and her husband Paul had boarded a Philippine Airlines flight in San Francisco with first class tickets to Manila. When they realized they were the only passengers in the first-class cabin, both became anxious about their decision to undertake this new assignment.

Just before takeoff, a Filipino man dressed in a bright Hawaiian shirt and sandals came on board holding a cocktail in one hand and stack of magazines in the other. He noisily walked down the aisle giving orders to the flight attendants in what they assumed to be one of the many Philippine languages.

In excellent English, he spoke to Laura and Paul, introduced himself and stated that he had been too long in the states and was eager to get home. He showed little interest in the American couple or why they were headed to Manila.

When the seatbelt sign went off, Laura got up and walked to where their fellow passenger was seated. "My husband and I are curious why so few passengers are on such a large plane," she said. "Since it is the only flight to the Philippines today, we expected it to be was filled with Filipinos going home."

He shrugged his shoulders and responded by pointing to a curtain at the end of the aisle of their first-class section. Laura walked back, opened the curtain and found the other passengers. Three cramped seats ran down each side of a small aisle and were filled with the Filipino men, women, children and babies she had expected to see when she boarded. The flight would be a long one—sixteen hours to Manila. Two refueling stops were scheduled, but still Laura could imagine the discomfort the coach passengers would have on the trip.

On her return pass by the only Filipino in a decent seat, he gave a condescending shake of his head and grimace that indicated their cabin mate did not have a high opinion of his countrymen who were riding in coach.

Laura and the man did not speak again. She and Paul assumed this was not a pleasant journey for their traveling companion. The attendant kept him supplied with cocktails until he was fast asleep.

Why was a newly-retired Episcopal priest and a university professor and noted author headed to spend a year in a remote location in the Philippine Islands? Both Laura and Paul were also beginning to have doubts but not sharing their concerns. The year before, both had ended long and rewarding careers that had left little time to spend together in activities both enjoyed. Retirement was to have been that time. They'd spent three months in Europe, a month at a favorite beach, seen many Broadway shows, and visited family and friends. This was the retirement life they had anticipated. Both had felt satisfaction at the completion of careers spent actively involved in the duties of priest and teacher. Laura had always considered her writing as teaching—the same as being in the classroom.

Life had been pleasant and serene until Paul visited his mentor, a retired bishop now volunteering his time in the national church office of missions and relief. After exchanging pleasantries and catching up on their recent lives, the elder priest surprised Paul with a proposal. "How would you feel about being part of establishing a parish and church in a remote part of the world that is desperately needing a priest?" What first seemed like a rhetorical question brought a prolonged silence.

As the bishop waited, Paul realized this was a serious question and must be answered. "I appreciate you thinking of me, but I have no thoughts of pastoring a church again," said Paul. "In the future, I would enjoy short mission assignments. But, you know, I will go where the Lord leads me. Where is this parish?"

"On the island of Mindanao, in the Philippine Islands. I just returned from there. It is a beautiful place. Weather is pleasant year-round. The people are delightful. You would have a lovely home with orchids growing in your yard. There is a sound Anglican and Episcopalian group of ex-pats from the U.S., Canada, England, and Australia living in the area. They have petitioned the Bishop of Davao to start a mission in the area of Baslig." He handed Paul a map of Mindanao with the area highlighted in yellow.

Paul's interest was piqued enough that he wanted to know more. "Can they support a church?"

The bishop looked at him with a serious expression. "It will be a struggle, but there will be help from several sources. And sponsorship by the Diocese of Davao. Davao is the capital and largest city on Mindanao.

"These are strong church men and women who have chosen to make their home on the edge of civilization and desire a liturgical place to worship. They also have bonded strongly with the Filipino population and are a blessing in many ways."

"Tell me more about the native population. What religion do they practice? What are their lives like?" Paul could not imagine a church where the local population was not included.

"There is a minority Roman Catholic presence. Some practice pagan beliefs from their past, but a growing number have participated in Bible Studies led by the ex-pats. The worship service would need to be adapted to reach the needs of all.

"You would have the opportunity to do the intense mission work that you have always believed possible."

"Are there insurgent rebellions?" Paul had read reports of assaults on nuns in the Phillipines.

"A very small and peaceful group of that sect is in the area. The revolts have been in the extreme southern end of the island, around Zamboanga. There are many miles of dense jungle between the area of Baslig and the turmoil. The attacks are led by a small extremist faction—not the larger community."

Paul took a deep breath. "You are making this very tempting, but there is a lot to consider. You know, Laura and I have five children scattered around the U.S., and I can't keep up with the number of grandkids. We both want to be more closely involved in their lives."

"Planes fly every day, Paul. Think of the experience for your family to visit you. Of course, your stipend will not be anything like you have received in the past, but you will have little expense. By Filipino standards, you will be wealthy enough to buy many airplane tickets."

Paul sighed. "I'll think about it and talk with Laura, but it's very unlikely."

The bishop gazed at him for a moment. "Didn't you just say that you will go where the Lord leads you? That's all I'm asking."

A packet of information on the area and a copy of the petition for a church had been prepared before Paul had called and arranged to visit his friend. The visit had been prompted by concern for the bishop's health, but he could see now that his mentor had welcomed the opportunity to present the proposal to one of his most valued protégés.

Paul left with the packet under his arm, and a surprising new lightness in his step. *What will Laura think? Can I ask her to do this after she has devoted so much of her time to supporting my ministry? Why should I think of disrupting years ahead of this fulfilling life with Laura?* It was clear he had some praying to do.

Walking home from the train, Paul enjoyed the bracing coolness of early fall. It was his favorite time of year in New York. He had never lost his awe at the changing leaves of autumn.

Before entering the house, he loaded his arms with firewood and planned to have a cheery fire going when Laura returned from shopping in the city. He set out a fine bottle of red wine, and without thinking, he dropped the packet on the coffee table and went into the bedroom to change into his jeans and turtleneck.

As he finished pulling the shirt over his head, he heard her come into the house and call their cat. He slipped on loafers and hurried to give his wife the kiss he had been looking forward to all day.

His beautiful Laura had changed little since the first time he had looked into the bluest eyes he had ever seen. Her raven hair was beginning to be laced with gray, but he still marveled that someone so beautiful had become his wife.

She had spied the packet of information and already spread it out on the coffee table to look over when he came into the room. He stood silently until she finished scanning the material. He had planned to bring up later.

Laura knew the heart and soul of her Paul. She looked up and into his eyes, and with a suspicious giggle asked simply, "When do we leave?"

After three months of packing, visiting family, attending orientations about the country, celebrating Christmas and New

Years and many going-away parties, the new adventure to the wild, wild west of the Phillipines was before them.

Leaving their beloved home was less difficult when two of Laura's favorite students from Columbia University were delighted to move into the house, take care of any needs and best of all, become foster parents to Elizabeth V, the latest of a long line of cats all named Elizabeth in honor of Laura's grandmother.

＊＊＊

They took advantage of the luxury of first class, enjoyed the cocktails, gourmet meals and the comfort of sleep in the lay-back seats as they navigated through the darkness over the Pacific Ocean. Short stops for refueling were made on Hawaii and Wake Island, where first-class passengers were allowed to get out of the plane and stretch their legs.

As they stood waiting to reboard, Paul glanced at his wife, who seemed uncharacteristically quiet. "A penny for your thoughts," he said.

Laura looked back at him and smiled wistfully. "I've been thinking of the tales Uncle Woody told me about being in the South Pacific during World War II," she said. "He never told me any of those experiences until after Aunt Ruth died. He has been so lost and lonely without her. Maybe that is why his thoughts drift back to his Navy days." She paused before continuing. "I'm glad they moved back to Georgia when he retired. It's good for Aunt Laura James and him to live close together now that they are both alone."

The loss of her beloved Aunt Ruth and Uncle Carlton was still hard for Laura to accept. After the deaths of her father and then her mother, Grandma Myra and the rest of the MacTavish family had become her surrogate parents.

She changed the subject. "Honey, doesn't it seem strange that the passengers in coach weren't allowed off the plane?"

Paul nodded. "Yes, it does. I know they would benefit from a little fresh air and time out of their seats. I don't understand, but I know we'll be seeing a lot of things that we don't understand. Dorothy, you're not in Georgia anymore."

Laura playfully poked him. "Just shut up, you damn Yankee."

After leaving Wake Island, they spent the remaining flight watching the sun glittering off white cap waves. Paul moved across the aisle so both could have a window seat. Not long after, both exclaimed at the same time. "LOOK!" The island of Luzon had come into view.

Within minutes, the plane had landed. As they reached the open door of the plane, they were met by a shock wave of heat and humidity. Before they were allowed to walk onto the steps to exit the plane, their passports, visas, and identification were scrutinized by uniformed and armed soldiers.

This was not a surprise—they had been warned that the PC or army was in charge of all law enforcement on the islands. One of the soldiers pointed to a door on the right. "You go that way." They noticed that their Filipino cabin mate had been pointed to the door on the left.

Before reaching their door, they saw all of the coach passengers entering the left door also, and wondered why it seemed that the Filipino citizens were scrutinized more thoroughly than foreigners.

Later, Paul and Laura received the answers to both of their questions. They learned that the present head of state had enemies among his own countrymen, and that the credentials of Filipino citizens were examined for names on a list of those unfriendly to the president. Allowing the horde of coach passengers to leave the plane on the two stops along the way might give an enemy of the president opportunity to take the seat of a coach passenger and travel to Manila.

They entered a small room and were told to sit on a wooden bench and wait for their luggage to be brought. This was the first knowledge that their belongings would not be transferred to the connecting flight to Mindanao, and they would have to transport the bulky baggage to the next gate. Fortunately, they had followed the directives given for packing and had shipped a container of essential items, clothing, books, a supply of toiletries, cooking spices and specialties that would be unavailable on their new island home. Laura's backpack was filled to capacity with medicines and anything needed immediately. Paul's carry-on was a computer and printer. Sharing the computer would be hectic. Once they were settled a second could be ordered and shipped.

The luggage arrived just before their thirst became unbearable. Passing through customs went smoothly, and the agent was helpful and drew a rudimentary map of the route they should take to reach the gate of their flight to Mindanao.

Paul studied the map before leaving the helpful agent. First, he had to find a currency exchange. The agent was little help with this but assured them they would pass one somewhere. They felt comforted by their first and very pleasant experience with a Filipino.

They both shook his hand and said "*Salamat*," the only phrase they knew. They soon found that the Filipino word for "Thank you" would be the word they would use most frequently throughout their stay.

The agent gave them what they learned was a true Filipino smile and replied, " *Walay sapayan.*" They assumed correctly that this meant "You're welcome." This became a word they would use often also.

Fortunately, the customs agent was fluent in all the dialogues of the country. The only words they had practiced were in Visayan, the dialect of Mindanao, which was one of the many languages spoken in different locations.

They had much to learn. Thanks to the map and questions asked along the way they were able to find not only the correct gate for departure but currency exchange and bottled water. Morale improved to a pleasant level. The gate was a little concrete block building unattached to the main building. A multitude of, men, women, children and several small cages that seemed to carry animals stood outside the small structure. As soon as they reached the group, they were treated to more Filipino smiles, and a path opened for them to go inside the door of the building. "Salamat, Salamat, Salamat" was spoken to everyone they passed.

Inside the building was an equally large crowd of people and one person sitting at a table in front with a chalkboard for writing gate calls. Again, the smiling Filipinos provided an opening to two suddenly unoccupied spots beside a wall that would give back support. They did not refuse.

After a short rest and long drink of water, Paul spent the waiting time walking around the mass of Filipinos gathered at the gate, asking questions about the flight and making friends. A burden was lifted when he found that almost none were hesitant to converse in English. He learned that English was taught in all schools and marveled at their ability and willingness. How different from the US where immigrants who did not immediately speak English were sometimes resented.

This was the gate for several flights to areas of Mindanao. There was no set time for their flight to arrive. Many of the people surrounding the gate were not going on a flight but were family members saying farewell. The answer to "When can we expect the plane?" was "Must wait."

Everyone seemed to have unlimited patience in this knowledge. Children ran around, laughing and playing. The sound of chickens was heard, along with what might have been a baby goat. In their orientation before the trip, they were told to "Prepare for anything and don't get in a hurry. These are beautiful people." Everyone seemed to be in a festive mood. This was a moment when both Paul and Laura knew they were following a higher command.

With the sputter of a small plane, everyone—including Paul—raced for a look at the chalkboard. When "DAVOA" was written in large letters, wide Filipino smiles all turned to them and said, "Come, come."

Two men picked up their luggage and carried it to the plane. Behind them was a young fellow carrying a cage with several pigeons inside. That day they learned a phrase they would repeat throughout their stay. *Only in the Philippines.*

As the small plane taxied for takeoff, both Paul and Laura felt their tensions drain away. They had made it—well almost—to their new home. A love affair with the Filipino people had already begun in their hearts by the time they reached altitude. People chattering, children squealing, pigeons cooing and a baby goat baaing told them this would be a year filled with joy and peace.

Chapter II
2000

The little plane to Davao did not have the power or comfort of the jet they had flown across the Pacific Ocean. It sputtered and seemed to struggle to stay above the trees. Looking out the window, they saw only dense rainforest with tall tree tops forming a continuous canopy, ocean, and then more rainforest. The land below seemed endless with no sight of towns or people.

This last portion of their long flight was uncomfortably hot, and odors from the animals wafted through the small cabin. No one, including Paul and Laura, were perturbed. The passengers were a jolly group that chatted and questioned the American couple. When they learned that Paul was a priest, they were not sure how he should be addressed or how he should be treated. Several crossed themselves every time they spoke to him.

The flight from Manila to Davao would take three hours. No food was served but many of the passengers brought out lunches and offered to share with the Americans, but Laura and Paul politely refused.

Soon the cabin was fill with a strange and obnoxious stench. Laura leaned over and whispered to Paul. "Do you smell that awful odor? Is something wrong with the plane?"

"I don't think so, but I'm getting nauseous from the smell. It seems to be coming from what someone is eating. Smells like rotten garlic." Before Paul could say more, an uproar broke out a few seats back and several passengers converged on one man.

Loud, angry words were heard and the charged man was trying to hold onto what looked like a piece of fruit. His accusers said only one word—*durian*. The co-pilot hurried to the ruckus and demanded the man release the melon. Carrying the melon with its putrid stink, the co-pilot stopped beside the Americans to try to explain this strange phenomenon in English words they would understand. The fruit was forbidden in many places—especially on airplanes.

From their fellow passengers, they learned that durian was addictive for much of the population. Rumors reported that it had many claimed benefits, the most popular of which was that it was an aphrodisiac, or love potion. It was forbidden in all buildings and on all public transportation. Further explanation was unnecessary for the couple. The smell lingered in the plane.

After this one encounter with the odor of the durian, Laura and Paul had no interest in learning more. Combined with animal smells and sweaty perspiration, it made the cabin air unbearable. Many, including Laura, became ill.

Paul stood near the end of the flight and, after thanking them for sharing their country, he gave his standard Episcopal greeting. "The peace of the Lord be always with you."

Laura answered in turn, "And also with you." Everyone on the plane responded when she led them the second time. We must translate this into Visayan, thought Laura. Even though most speak English, it is a compliment when visitors speak your language.

After departing the little plane at Davao airport, the smell of the durian lingered on each passenger. The pilot grabbed the accused as he walked down the steps and marched him in to the authorities. A trial was not necessary—he had broken an essential law and would spend time in jail.

As promised, Laura and Paul were met by a British couple who had been instrumental in establishing a church in the area of Baslig. Both were excited to meet them but they kept a safe distance as soon as they smelled the durian.

"Our dear Vicar, we have looked forward to this moment throughout all of our time in this beloved country. We welcome you and your lovely wife to our home and our hearts. Plans are for dinner with the bishop, and we will spend tomorrow morning laying out plans for the future of our church.

"But first things first. We must get you to the hotel for a bath and shampoo. Best put your clothes in bags at the hotel and ask to have the entire lot burned. The hotel is very familiar with durian. No offense, old chap, but you stink!"

The couple, Nigel and Val Beasley, were strong Anglicans who had lived at this post for sixteen years while Nigel had been working for a forestry company. The four quickly bonded on the ride to the hotel. Much laughter and joking was exchanged about the smell of American Episcopalians. A long soak in tub, hair shampooed and fresh clothes from luggage that had not encountered the durian erased any misgivings they Paul and Laura might have felt about the plane ride.

Sitting on the terrace of one of Davao's luxury resorts, sipping a cool, tall, fruity rum punch, and nibbling on a tray of local delicacies as they looked at the moon above the Pacific Ocean waters of the Bay of Davao removed any further doubts about their decision. The bishop and his wife, both Americans from Pennsylvania, were open, welcoming, and easy to immediately love.

Laura was overwhelmed at their beautiful, colorful clothing. Nigel and the bishop wore light trousers with the native barong shirts made from thin pineapple fiber and embroidered down the front. The bishop added a stiff clerical collar, but his attire was as relaxed as that of the rest of the welcoming party. The ladies wore long skirts with colorful embroidered flowers around the hem and blouses similar to the material of the barongs.

"I had no idea of the type of clothing to bring and now know I will need a new wardrobe. Tell me how and where to find this beautiful local clothing." Laura felt quite prim and uncomfortable in her "professor attire" of tailored pants and blouse. More appropriate clothing for her and for Paul was a must. Both ladies assured her that they had arrived with the same type clothing and had immediately learned that "cool and loose" were the criteria for clothes in the tropics.

Val Beasley was delighted to assist her new neighbor. "There are lovely local and Chinese fabrics available in shops in the barrio, as well as gifted seamstresses who will make outfits to suit your taste," she said. "I will go with you until you learn the ropes. You will be surprised at the beautiful wardrobe you can acquire for a small number of pesos, and when you translate pesos into dollars, you will marvel at the amount. Our problem is acquiring too many clothes since it is such fun to visit the fabric shops and seamstress."

The bishop looked at Paul. "You are probably in better shape. Short pants are usually worn daily...with a loose shirt. You should get a few barongs for occasions. I suggest wearing your stole over a white or colorful barong shirt according to the occasion. Of course, you can fit in your clerical collar."

Nigel gave the vicar a "leg up" to avoid embarrassing mistakes. "Remember, old chap, protocol is necessarily quite different in the rain forest than Staten Island."

Dinner was served in courses and as delicious as that found in a five-star restaurant. Both Paul and Laura were warned not to get too attached to this style of dining. In the remote area of Baslig, their new friends told them, the food would not be as varied or as plentiful.

After the heavy meal with coffee and brandy on the terrace, they found their comfortable room to be paradise—the ocean breeze blew through windows opened wide.

Paul was up for an early breakfast and morning meeting with the bishop and Nigel. There was much to discuss, and little time to cover all that Paul felt necessary. He was most anxious to start the journey to Baslig.

Laura enjoyed the leisure of sleeping later, breakfast with her new friends, and a long chat on the terrace. She and Paul would leave at noon in the Beasley's small Japanese car with an ice chest of bottled water, fruit and sandwiches for the four-hour trip.

Chapter III
2000

The little orange Datsun provided a swerving but otherwise comfortable ride along the shore of the gulf of Davao and then onto hard-packed dirt bordering the rain forest. The necessity of the small car was recognized as they maneuvered the narrow winding road. Paul wondered what would happen if a vehicle approached to pass. That soon occurred and with a lot of maneuvering and skill, both vehicles were able to continue on their route.

"I haven't seen a Datsun in a long time. In the U.S., these are called Nissans now." Paul was impressed with the speed and agility of the small auto on the narrow, curvy and sometime washboard road. Few cars passed, but each time was a tight squeeze.

Nigel nodded. "You will see many here. This car is best for our roads. Most, like this one and the one you will be receiving, are ancient. The odometer has turned over many times. We keep them in excellent running condition with local mechanics who understand their purpose." He paused for a moment, looking in the rearview mirror.

"There are rumors that Nissan will start producing Datsuns again for a limited market, but I wouldn't trade my 'orange marvel' for anything."

Paul shook his head. "I don't know how proficient my driving will be, but I *will* need to purchase some means of transportation."

"You'll get the knack quickly. Our little group of churchmen were fortunate to have a small Datsun truck donated to us by a friend who was returning to Australia. It should serve your needs...unless you were planning on a BMW."

Paul chuckled at this because he had never driven a luxury car of any kind. "Perfect," he said. "I especially like having a truck."

Laura was intrigued at the sights along the rainforest side of the road. In several clearings, small homes made of bamboo with nepa roofs were surrounded by animals and people.

Each time they passed a clearing, Nigel slowed down and waved, and children raced to the car. A tradition was immediately evident when Nigel placed candy in each outstretched hand. "Salamat, Salamat," said the children with big Filipino smiles.

They passed a group of ladies walking beside the road balancing huge baskets on their heads. Laura's camera was clicking away. When an enormous water buffalo approached with a young boy riding astride him, Nigel stopped the car for Laura and Paul to stand beside him and pose for a photo.

I must have copies made of this to send back home and show our new life, thought Laura. I will never go out again without a supply of candy and a camera. She could feel excitement bubbles running through her veins, and remembered her Grandma Myra saying, "Oh, how proud I am to be here."

In the mid-point of their trip, Nigel left the road and pulled over under a shade of palms. "How about we stretch our legs and have a bite of lunch? And, ladies if necessary, this is a proper place to step into the brush."

Although Nigel's clipped British words made a toilet break sound quite formal, Laura looked at the thicket and wondered if she could hold out for the rest of the trip. Noises coming through the brush were like the soundtrack of a Tarzan movie. But, there would be no Shell Oil station or McDonalds further down the road, so the only choice was to follow Val, who cleared back the brush for Laura to enter.

After the safe return of the ladies, they ate cold fish sandwiches, sliced mango, papaya and two fruits Laura had never seen before. Each drank two bottles of cool water.

"I see why you have chosen this to be your home, Val," said Laura. "After being here only one day, I would find it hard to leave." Val and Nigel laughed as if she had discovered a secret.

After the picnic, they made a turn to the east and onto a road much wider and smoother for the drive to Baslig. When they were passed by several large log trucks, they realized why the road had improved. They were nearing the lumber mills.

Their approach into Baslig took them through the barrio and up a small mountain to their new home. They had no idea what to expect. Would it be a nepa hut?

Nigel started to explain as they began to see modest but adequate homes made of concrete blocks and painted pastels.

"These homes were built for the ex-pat supervisors of the paper mill that was built here. It is a lovely spot to live, out of the dusty paths and cooler than below. I find this quite a comfortable and pleasant home."

"So, we will be neighbors." This pleased Laura. "Tell more about the people leaving the houses. Who lives here now?"

Val took over explaining. "The paper mill could have been very successful, but during the early time of martial law, the ex-pats who were here to train their Filipino counterparts were sent away. The mill floundered and finally closed, which took away the best chance of employment for the people of the barrio. Some of the ex-pats stayed on and found other employment, but mainly the homes are occupied by folks in forestry liked Nigel. There are a few artists and writers, and some retirees."

"So how do we pay for our home?" Paul had only been told a home would be provided.

"My, my, you look a gift horse in the mouth, old chap. The lovely home that you will inhabit was owned by a Canadian couple who lived there for many years and made a beautiful garden. They grew old and the wife died. Shortly after, the husband died too. They were a devoted couple and did everything together, even dying.

When their son came over to settle the estate, we learned they had left the home to be used as a vicarage. They were devoted to having a church established here, but sadly did not live to see you arrive." Nigel eyes filled with tears.

Paul shook his head in amazement. "I wish I could have known them. What a blessing they have left for us. We surely must place something in the church in their memory and honor." Paul made that a vow.

The little Datsun passed a curve and came to a stop in front of a lime green cottage with a tiled roof. "Welcome to our vicarage and your home," Nigel said with pride.

During the tour of the completely furnished and spacious home, something rubbed against Laura's leg. "Oh, there's an animal in here!"

Val chuckled. "It's a tradition when residents return to their home countries, they leave behind a house cat who becomes the property of the next occupant." Val picked up a large gray tabby and nuzzled her before handing her over to Laura.

Laura looked into the cat's eyes and cooed to her. "Oh, sweet kitty, you are just like my Elizabeth Five that I had to leave behind. I love you."

The cat curled up in her arms and started purring. Now their life in this faraway land was complete.

Chapter IV
2000

After a tour of the house, Val opened the refrigerator to show a bottle of white wine, a bowl of shrimp salad, and sliced fruit for their dinner. Then the Beasleys left Laura and Paul to get acquainted with their new home.

Each step revealed a new delight. Every room was completely furnished—including linens and towels. There was even a supply of cat food.

For their first meal on the terrace of their new home, Laura lit candles and set the perfect supper on the table. Both sat in the glow of the candles and sniffed the aromas wafting through the air that were both flowery and fruity. Had they arrived in Eden?

Elizabeth Six continually moved between laps. They seemed to be the family she had been awaiting.

Paul grabbed both of his wife's hands and looked deeply into her blue, blue eyes. "Babe, do you know how I feel tonight?"

"Tell me."

"The first night I was invited to come into your apartment in New York we sat on the terrace and shared Elizabeth One sitting in our laps, I felt so full of joy and thought never would anything match that feeling. But here we are tonight, and I just want to shout out my joy and how much I love you and how thankful I am for your love…and understanding of this humble servant of the Lord."

Laura eased Elizabeth Six to the floor, and joined Paul in his chair. "Thank you, my darling" were the only words that fit. They cuddled and kissed like young lovers until both broke out laughing because Elizabeth Six had joined them and was trying to establish a spot for herself.

Paul spoke with a mock seriousness. "No offense to Grandmother Elizabeth, but there is one thing I am not comfortable with and want to change."

"What on earth?" At that moment, Laura would not have changed anything.

"The name Elizabeth Six just does not fit this kitty. I will not make her stand up to the standards of decorum set for her by the Elizabeths. She is a jungle babe, and henceforth her name shall be Lizzy."

"Let me think," said Laura. "How 'bout her proper name remains Elizabeth Six and we just *call* her Lizzy?"

Paul laughed. "Once again, you have maneuvered me into a compromise. Let's clear the table and try our new bed."

"I do think that is the best proposition I've had in Mindanao."

Laura looked for Lizzy to be sure she was safely inside, but she had disappeared. A frantic search began until Paul called out, "Here she is. She has already taken her place on our bed. I'd say this is a true cat of faith."

Laura chuckled. "Thank you, Father Paul."

Morning broke with sunbeams and light breezes filling their bedroom. No time to linger in bed—there was much to begin. Coffee, croissants and fruit was in the kitchen for a breakfast on the terrace. Both declared it as good as a New York bagel with cream cheese and jam.

Before departing the night before, Nigel had explained the plans for the first day. "I think it is time to address you correctly since we will gather with the others of our group. As the bishop told you, Father Paul, the diocese has rented a vacant store front in the barrio for us to gather. Shall I stop for you at nine o'clock? Your newly refurbished vehicle should be ready by the end of our meeting. We had it inspected and repaired as needed."

Paul's voice was trembling with excitement. Holding services in a storefront had been one of his hidden desires since entering the priesthood. "Sounds great—our first vestry meeting."

Val had turned to Laura. "Would you prefer to join the gathering or would you like a tour of the barrio, market and some instructions on shopping? I can introduce you to the fabric shop owner and the seamstress, and we haven't even mentioned servants for you. You will need two maids and a houseboy."

Laura was astonished at the mention of servants at all, much less three! Ruby had been her housekeeper, cook and caretaker of the children when necessary. After the children were in school, Ruby had retired and moved back to Georgia. A cleaning service had visited the house once a week and everyone else pitched in to do other chores.

Laura and Paul wanted their children to learn the work ethic of Grandma Myra and have responsibilities. Now with only the two of them living in a much smaller house, she had not planned on any outside helpers. Also, the word "servant" gave her an uncomfortable feeling.

"I do need and want your help in learning how to shop in the barrio. Paul, would you like me to attend the meeting?" He shook his head to say no. She knew he would give her a thorough description of everything that happened.

She turned to Val. "I had not planned to have any outside help. It will be a joy to take care of our new home, and we both love to cook."

Val giggled. "I am sure you would do this in your home in the states, but you must understand that it is far different here. First, you need a houseboy to bring water from the spring every day to fill the cistern. Your drinking water should be bottled, but spring water for bathing and cleaning must be added to the rainwater cistern as needed.

"And he will have much work to do in the yard and garden every day. Everything grows so fast that you and Paul could never keep up with it. Your home would be covered with vines very soon."

Laura understood as she remembered the battles with kudzu vines spreading in Georgia.

"Servants are a must to do your shopping and washing as well as cleaning the house. They know how to pick the best food items and bargain in the market."

"Wouldn't one maid be sufficient?"

"Possibly, but no servant will stay here alone. Without company, Filipinos are very lonely and likely to leave."

"Stay *here*? We can't accommodate two extras in our small house!"

"That is the purpose of the small room on the back of the house with the outside door. Filipinos live in much smaller huts, and there is room for a bed and also a small toilet."

Paul had already appropriated this room as his office and especially liked having a toilet that could be used by visitors. He would be very disappointed. "I will try having one helper other than the houseboy, but wouldn't she be happy just coming for the day?" Laura continued to avoid the word "servant."

Val was astonished, as newcomers usually were delighted to have as much help as available for them. "You are sure?"

Laura nodded and said, "I will make it work."

"I know two sisters who need work and are from a very dependable family. Would you like to talk with them?"

And that became the plan.

The morning after their arrival, Val picked Laura up in her own little yellow Datsun. In the barrio, she parked in the street, and they walked from shop to shop on the planks that covered the muddy street past all the shops all the way to the market. As they walked, an expanding group of women and children gathered near.

Laura was intrigued by the crowd. "Is something happening that is bringing all of these people to the barrio? They seem to be following our every step."

"You'll get accustomed to having them stare at you. Ignore them." Val brushed off the question as though it was an everyday occurrence.

"Why do they want to stare at us? It feels rude to ignore them."

"Word of your arrival has spread. They've come to see the new American lady." Val laughed at the expression on Laura's face. "If it will make you feel more at ease, say, *Maayong buntag*. That is 'good morning' in Visayan."

With her still Southern accent, Laura said, "Maayong buntag" over and over until she had covered all her admirers. And, she had added another word to her vocabulary.

The first tour of the market taught Laura that she did indeed need help with the shopping. It was a matter of pushing and shoving through the market and searching out what you desired. The two large baskets Val had brought for their purchases filled quickly. With assistance, Laura selected any fruits and vegetables that she recognized—eggs, canned milk, rice, and a chicken. She was abashed at how she would put this together into a meal. Yes, I do need help with the cooking and a Philippine cookbook—could I order it online?

They finished the barrio excursion at noon and walked further down the dusty street to the storefront church headquarters. She was surprised to see the room filled with the men and women who would be the communicants of Paul's parish. All of them were delighted to meet her and expressed a hearty welcome.

Hearing the different accents mingle as they discussed their hopes for the success of their parish was heartening. Aside from being strong leadership for the church, they would all become dear and helpful friends.

A lunch of cold chicken, fruits, pasta salad, spring rolls, and fruit punch was spread out for a noon meal. Afterwards, they dispersed to their homes and a traditional afternoon siesta.

Another lesson was learned. The ex-pats adapted to life by following the traditions of the native folks: Food is usually provided at any gathering and is served cold. Much energy is spent walking and carrying out the morning agenda, so in the hottest part of the day, a rest is necessary. Laura and Paul came to the same conclusion and soon relished their own siesta.

After the meeting, they left with an Australian couple, Rhonda and Russell, and picked up their truck, which had been stored in a garage. When the Australians left them, they said, "G'day mates. Want you over for a barbie soon."

Laura climbed into their "new" truck. "I could listen to these different accents forever," she said. "They seem to have all been away from their homeland a long time, but the accents are as distinct as ever." Being an English professor and writer had made Laura much attuned to language.

Paul smiled. "I don't know whether I prefer being called 'chap' or 'mate,' but I guess they both translate as 'friend.'"

"How 'bout y'all?" said Laura, and she gave him another "damn Yankee" punch.

The little red Datsun truck shone and drove like brand new even though it was obviously ancient. It was perfect for the narrow, curvy roads and frequent stops for someone on a water buffalo or a group of Filipinos strolling leisurely.

Everyone stopped to watch them pass. They waved and chanted an assortment of greetings which Laura and Paul did not understand. But they knew they were being welcomed. Both smiled, waved and replied using Laura's newly acquired Visayan "Maayong buntag."

This was followed by a cheerful laugh from the group being addressed. Later, she learned that they were saying, "Good morning" in the afternoon. The phrase in the afternoon should be "Maayong hapon" and at night, "Maayong gabi."

When they reached the house, they saw Val's car in front. She was sitting cross-legged on the walkway with two young Filipino girls. Laura had forgotten that she had to make a decision on employing a helper.

Val introduced the girls by their first names, Lupe and Inez. Both looked about fourteen. It would be a hard decision for Laura, but she did not think she needed two helpers in her house and she did not want live-in help.

Their command of English was scattered. Laura could only say "Thank you," "You're welcome," and "Good morning."

With the help of Val, they were able to explain that the girls would take turns working through the day and go home in the evening. They shook their heads and spoke Visayan directly to Val, which Laura took to mean they were not pleased with the arrangement. Assuring them their pay would be the same as if they were staying day and night made no difference to them.

"Laura," said Val, "they would be heartbroken not to be able to work for you. They are willing to work all day and go home in the evening *if* they are allowed to take their daily allotment of rice home to share with the family and can freely take the coconuts that fall from your trees."

This request baffled Laura, but she was certainly willing for them to have both if this was of value to the girls. Both beamed ear-to-ear smiles when Val assured them the benefit of rice and coconuts would be the same as if both were staying day and night. Of course, Laura became immediately attached to the girls but was concerned that they were so young. "Shouldn't they be in school?" she asked.

Another lesson. Filipinos have a youthful appearance, Val told her, until they are well into their forties. The two girls were 23 and 26 years old. Both were married and each had several children. Sharing the work days was ideal since there would always be one sister at home with the children. Laura felt relieved and knew this relationship would be good for all.

There was no need to hire a houseboy. The same man had worked for the previous owners for many years and had been continuing to keep the house and grounds in good order. The next day when they met Qurino, they found he was a house*man* and not a boy. When asked his age, he could not tell them, but he remembered when the Japanese came and his family hid out in caves in the mountains and ate monkeys."

With a toothless smile, he said, "Then GIs come and give Hershey Bars." He was so possessive over the house and yard, Laura knew he would let nothing go undone.

Chapter V
2000

Paul and Laura arrived in their new home in early February, one of the most pleasant months of the tropical seasons. In the Phillippines, spring, summer, autumn and winter have no meaning. The climate is divided into wet and dry.

Their first experiences were a vacationer's dream—comfortably cooled by the balmy breezes and dry except for occasional showers in the late afternoon. There was always humidity because of the proximity to seas all around but it was not as oppressive as during the hot wet season. No matter what time of year, flowers and trees were always green and blooming.

Laura checked the first morning, and orchids were growing as parasites on the many palm trees in her back yard. She had long had a fascination with orchids—in her homes in the past, she had struggled to pamper orchid plants but none had lived beyond its first blooms. Now her yard was glorified with orchids of all sizes and colors that prospered with no assistance at all from her.

Colorful flowers were always in bloom in the yards of their neighbors no matter what the season, and since they'd arrived, Laura had searched every yard for rose bushes, finding none. She had hope of finding a catalogue that could ship a few bushes to her—the gazebo in their back yard, she thought, would be perfect for some climbing roses. What a lovely setting for she and Paul to sit in late afternoon and enjoy the smell of their roses.

She went to Val, her most reliable source of information, and asked for help in finding rose bushes to plant.

Val answered with her usual British candor. "Roses do not grow here." Her tone and answer took Laura by surprise for a moment. Then she realized that with all the beauty and nature surrounding her, how ungrateful she was to ask for one more flower!

The first weeks were hectic for Paul but luxurious for Laura. He spent long hours at the storefront and used his siesta time to plan sermons and activities. Services were to be held in the storefront each Sunday, and Eucharist celebrated Wednesday evenings. Add to that meetings to plan the church building and determine the role of the Filipino population. Any unscheduled time found Paul visiting the surrounding villages. The little red truck became well known in the huts on the rim of the rainforest.

Laura rode with him often and quickly found her heart filled with love for these simplistic, caring, lovely people. She searched for roles where her skills would be an asset. Giving out candy was rewarding but not lasting.

What can I do? she asked herself. I'm a teacher and writer, but I am also the granddaughter of Myra McTavish. She always told me to follow my heart—but where will it lead?

Laura had arrived on Mindanao with a preconceived heartache for the plight of the people she would meet. Her heart had always reached out to the "Least of These." Early childhood experiences with discrimination and Jim Crow customs were permanently etched on her heart.

Past mission visits with Paul had taken them to areas of extreme need in third-world areas and many parts of New York City. In every place, along with the need of basic necessities and opportunity of hope for a better life, was the need for dignity, simple respect.

She had expected the same from the smiling brown faces that greeted her. Their lifestyle offered little materially. Food was sparse. Homes were simple and small. Employment paid only a few pesos. Early death, especially to children, was a constant happening and often from an accident or a preventable illness.

These beautiful people already had dignity and an indomitable spirit of hope. They freely offered friendship. They were giving and sharing even though they had so little.

Neither bare walls, folding tables, and an assortment of chairs nor the challenge of reaching out to an entirely different congregation had discouraged Paul. He felt the excitement of his ex-pat parishioners who had only received communion as guests in a distant parish.

When he had prepared for his first service he needed assistance from anyone with time to contribute. Paul objected to suggestions of painting the walls and adding tile flooring to the storefront, since it would only be used a short time until the church was built. Plans for the church were well underway.

Land away from the congested barrio had been purchased by the diocese long before a priest had been secured. The walk from barrio to the church would be a pleasant stroll, and a collection of nepa huts were clustered nearby.

With the help of many eager parishioners, the shabby storefront was ready for the first service with chairs arranged in two semi-circles, with a prayer book and hymnal on each chair and a folding table covered by a donated white table cloth serving as an altar. A donated porcelain plate and large mug would serve as chalice and paten. A basket would hold the bread and wine would be poured straight from the bottle.

There would even be music. The organist of the Staten Island church had taped fifty hymns that Paul had requested.

On that first service in the storefront, Laura was as nervous as she had been on her wedding day. Two large fans blew a cross breeze, and like all others attending, her hair was a windblown snarl. She had no complaint because the strong breeze kept her cool as the skirt of her thin cotton dress swirled around her legs.

Her responsibility was the music. She had made several computer files to use during today and future services. It was a new delight to be able to select the music.

First came a prelude of familiar hymns as two young Filipino lads solemnly lit candles in wine bottles. Laura wondered who the lads were and how had they been trained as acolytes? She was baffled, as she had been many times by her husband and his reliance on the will of God.

After a short pause in the music, "All Things Bright and Beautiful" filled the little storefront now decked out in the finery of worship. The processional entered following a wooden cross that had been hastily made by an Australian parishioner.Paul followed wearing black trousers and a long-sleeved white shirt with his stole draped around his neck. He looked as priestly as he did at any service he had ever conducted. Nigel Beasley followed Paul for he would read the lessons.

The two very solemn Filipino acolytes processed to the front. A chair was beside the altar for the reader, but the barefoot acolytes sat cross-legged on the floor.

Laura marveled. How can I ever describe this perfect beginning with friends and family back home? she wondered.

Paul faced the congregation that totaled nine, counting Laura. Before beginning the rites of the service, he said, "I see we have an inquiring group standing outside. Rupert, would you please invite them to join us?"

Three Filipino women and two men came inside and sat cross-legged on the floor in front of the back wall. The remainder of the group continued to stand outside. From that first service forward, the little church which was so far unnamed offered a Sunday church service, a Wednesday evening Eucharist, a Sunday afternoon Bible class for children led by Laura and other ladies, an adult Bible class and a breakfast on Friday mornings. Each service continually grew and filled with Anglican ex-pats from neighboring areas. Many Filipinos first came for curiosity but returned because they felt welcomed and loved.

The time finally arrived to give the future church a name. The bishop and two parishioners arrived a few weeks after the first service to assist. When Paul was asked for his thoughts, he did not hesitate to share the name that he believed told the story of a place of worship in this outpost.

"My dear bishop," he said. "I would like for the name of our place of worship to represent our unique setting, our people and our hope for service. I suggest the parish be named the Church of the Holy Nativity on Mindanao.

The bishop smiled contentedly. "Yes, Father Paul, I agree. That is how this sanctuary should be consecrated, as a sacred place of worship born on Mindanao for all in the barrio and the rainforest and on the mountain." The bishop suggested that he return for a service of consecration in a few weeks after verification through diocesan channels.

Telephone calls were limited to local service. Long distance had to be patched into Manila via ham radio operators. This disturbed Laura because she had depended on communications with her family. She was told not to worry as ham radios were owned by most of the ex-pats and all had contacts in Manila.

On Friday afternoon, Paul received a call that a large shipping crate had arrived for him at the port. He sped the little Datsun down, down the steep incline to the port. Laura would be delighted to get the rest of their belongings from home.

With assistance, he heaved the heavy wooden box onto the back of the little truck. He did not recognize the crate as the one they had shipped—but assumed that he was confused, as that had been more than a month before.

There was no way he and Laura could lift the crate, so he pried open the crate and unpacked it in the bed of the truck.

The first item was inside a second box and padded with tissue paper. Both Laura and Paul gasped when it turned out to be a long piece of fair linen embroidered at the corners and center with crosses.

Other securely wrapped gifts were vessels needed for the Eucharist, candlesticks, and a sanctuary lantern. All were made of pottery—as silver would have been impractical. In the bottom of the box were a dozen prayer books and hymnals—a gift of the parish of Paul's church on Staten Island.

On top of the books was a carefully-wrapped package containing two candle snuffers. This brought tears and a long embrace between the couple. A letter enclosed carried the names of the staff of the Greenwich Village Mission where Laura and Paul had first met. It was signed by familiar names of the homeless souls who had dined there.

The little storefront stood in the middle of a teeming barrio on the edge of the rainforest, but the traditional decorum of the Anglican and Episcopal Church would have a sacred presence.

Laura and Paul were so moved by these meaningful gifts that the hugs, tears and dancing around was hard for them to stop. If neighbors had been looking, they might have questioned if their new priest was holding a pagan rite.

Laura was a believer in signs, and this surely was an encouragement. "Paul, never question your decision to answer this call to the jungle. Now you know you have a ministry here."

Paul kicked the side of the sturdy packing crate and laughed as he said, "And they even sent an altar." After a quick trip to the barrio for supplies, he spent the evening securing the crate, sanding and applying a coat of sealer that allowed the natural wood to show. It would look grand when covered with the fair linen, displaying the Eucharist vessels.

The first three months passed rapidly even though days were long and included time for rest and social visits. Both Laura and Paul found their activities kept them occupied except for the long noon-time siesta. The type of entertainment all expats had found in their former homes did not exist. This void was filled with social gatherings which included dinner, music, games, sometimes dancing and good conversation. It was a lovely, fulfilling life.

Since Laura had taken on responsibilities in the church and visits to the barrio, she was thankful to have the help with the house and yard that she had refused. Each morning Inez or Lupe was sitting beside the front door when Paul walked out to greet the new sunrise. Quietly and effortlessly, they ensured that delicious coffee was brewed and an array of fruits, croissants and cheese awaited Paul and Laura on the patio.

If Laura started to lift the coffee pot to pour a cup, one of the "helpers"—Laura could not bring herself to call these beautiful ladies "servants" or "maids"—would shake their heads and say, "I will be the one."

This happened for their every need, not only in the home but also in the barrio. It was as though every Filipino's joy was assisting the foreigners. This seemed awkward to Laura and Paul at first, but they realized it was insult to reject the help offered by these proud people.

Their home was spotless even though they never actually saw either helper at work. Windows were never closed except for rain. Since they were in a high elevation, cool breezes ventilated the rooms and brought in the flower scents to join the smell of sweet coconut oil used to polish the floors and furnishings. Their clothes were handwashed in spring water and dried quickly in the soft breezes. Since all clothes were cotton, a lot of ironing had to be done, yet clean, delightfully smelling clothes just seemed to magically appear each day.

Paul left in early morning for the storefront and would be involved in church affairs until noon lunch and siesta. Laura accompanied Lupe or Inez to the barrio to select foods for their meals every morning except Sunday. She wanted to learn to do this on her own but did not trust herself since the helper with her always knew the freshest and highest quality in fruits, vegetable or meats. Fresh fish, shrimp, or crab was usually the choice of the day.

The well-attended services and flow of people into the storefront chapel was giving Paul second thoughts about erecting an edifice of worship on land outside of the barrio.

He was conflicted between the ideals of establishing an Anglican designed church and moving away from the center of life for the people who now outnumbered the original sponsoring ex-pats. His first charge from the bishop, endorsed by the founding parishioner was to offer a faith that was open and welcoming to all. An attractive, more comfortable building would appeal to the ex-pats, but would eliminate the accessibility to life in the barrio.

He walked the muddy barrio streets each day and encountered needs that could best be filled by the gospel of a cup of clean water. From his daily encounters with Filipinos and practicing his lists of words, he was becoming more able to converse in Visayan. He made more friends by struggling to learn their language than by attempting traditionally to save their souls. He was addressed as "Padre of the Barrio" by most that he met.

Even the ex-pats picked it up but shortened it to Padre Barrio, which he relished. Filipinos had first dropped into the services from curiosity. They did not understand the sermons delivered in English but seemed to relate to the prayers and hymns. Since most of the ex-pats were also fluent in Visayan, prayers and lessons were partly done in the language of Mindanao.

Similarly, the Bible story class conducted by Laura relied on ex-pat wives to explain further. Instead of using Visayan completely, they believed that hearing the English words spoken by Laura gave a more sacred tone, and that turned out to be true. When the children began to say "Our Father" in English, they knew their approach had been meaningful.

Like her grandmother Myra, Laura was a gifted storyteller and made the biblical tales come alive with her accents and motions. The children were fascinated and were often heard acting out the stories—David and the giant, Joseph and his multi-colored coat, Jonah and the whale—all in a dialogue of mixed Visayan and English. Any disputes among the children were quickly settled by the phrase, "Do unto others..."

Paul found a young man to guide him on visits to the small villages bordering the rain forest. They drove as near as possible, left the little truck parked, and walked to the villages. When he heard the chattering noises in the bush and used his bolo knife to chop a path to a clearing, his memories returned to the Tarzan movies he had seen as a boy. There he found several nepa huts surrounding a communal center. Goats and chickens roamed freely.

He was welcomed by people and followed by a swarm of barefoot, near-naked children. He found families living in lean-tos made of bamboo and palm boughs. The barrio nepa homes were palaces compared to these villages.

He found it amazing that, even so, there were no complaints, begging or even distress with their lives. The people were generous, and he came home filled by the simplicity of trust and brotherly love—and a variety of bananas and mangos.

There was no employment, but their basic needs of food and shelter were met. If a storm blew their home away, another could be easily built. A limited variety of vegetables could be grown with only a simple tool to dig. The fertile land and rainfall provided growth.

This seeming Eden was offset by the high mortality rate from simple diseases and maladies, especially among the children. He had heard the term, "Life is cheap in the Third World" but had misinterpreted the meaning. The lives of loved ones was as dear in the rainforest as anywhere, but it was accepted that children would die from lack of health care and poor nutrition; fathers could be killed by falling from the top of a tree trying to shake down the valuable coconuts; and mothers might die from primitive childbirth.

Life was precarious in the barrio, the rainforest, and in the ghettos of New York. The only difference was accessibility of aid.

Back in the comfort of his cool and comfortable home, Paul found his mind and heart troubled. Laura knew this without any discussion, but she also knew that Paul needed to talk this out with someone other than her. When he left in the evening to sit alone in the dark, humid, storefront chapel, she did not question. She was concerned because he slept so little and had lost his robust appetite.

After several troubled weeks for both of them, he walked into the house whistling and smiling. "I've got it. I've got it. We can't do everything for everyone in this vast wild country, but we can do some things for many.

"God did not lead me to Mindanao to turn all of the people into Anglican suburbanites but to share the love of God. I can do this best by respecting their culture and sharing their friendship as a visible presence in the barrio and in the villages. There is much that we can do, but they know better how to walk in their shoes than I." Paul paused a moment to listen for Laura to say, "or in their bare feet."

"With God's help, we can do anything. He did not bring us here on a vacation to give thoughtful sermons and provide an Anglican environment to a few folks. He brought all of us, the ex-pats, you, and me to serve everyone."

Laura had not interrupted until he finished his declaration. Tears streamed down both of their glistening faces as she fell into his arms.

"Yes, we can. Yes, we can. We must first learn from them and then we can work on teaching. It's as simple as Education 101."

The next evening the entire ex-pat community was invited to their home for an impromptu barbecue. Inez was dismissed early for Paul to grill seafood and fruit kabobs to combine with the mixed salad Laura had learned to prepare with the leaf lettuce she had planted in their back yard.

After topping off everyone's coffee for a third time, and adding a splash of Frangelica, Paul was eager to discuss his thoughts, but when he looked around the room at his relaxed communicants he almost changed his mind. Laura gave him an encouraging smile, and he began. "I am so thankful for the start our parish has made so far, and I have all of you to thank."

The group looked comfortable, ready to enjoy an accounting of the successes of the past three months. But when he made the next statement, all sat up and became alert.

"I must confess," he said, "that I feel troubled that we are not headed in the direction of serving the most pressing needs."

There was no need to describe this further for all of the gathering had lived on Mindanao much longer than the new rector and knew the population and hardships well, but no one interrupted as he continued. He described his dilemma of making plans for building a structure outside of the barrio, his gospel of a cup of clean water, and the idea of bringing more people to Christ by respecting their culture than by first attempting to "save their souls."

When he finished, there seemed to be no accord. He was fearful of the response of those who had brought him to be their rector and establish a church.

Nigel Beasley who had been his staunchest supporter and close friend since the day he had arrived in Davao, cleared his throat.

"Padre Barrio, what I gather is that you have concluded that we should take the money appropriated for the permanent church structure and use it for mosquito netting, better housing in the rain forest, birth control practices and such, and show our brotherly love by remaining in the barrio."

Laura had never before heard Paul stammer and at a loss for words, but he was searching to convey his heartfelt thought.

Next to speak was the Australian, Russell Wynn. "Paul, how far would our resources for building a church reach? Do you realize the size of this island? It is an island but larger than many countries. You have only visited the edges of the rain forest.

"The interior is even more primitive, and what about the Sulu Archipelago and Zamboanga? We will help, and we *have* helped, but we have to be realistic of just how far our help can reach."

The perky British voice of Kim, a recent bride and new resident, broke the tension. "Zamboanga...isn't that where the monkeys have no tails?" This was a popular marching song of U.S. infantry written by Gsavoa in Cuba.

Laughter filled the room and one of the Americans said, "Yes, but that is just one of those things no amount of aid can change." Kim laughed along with them and realized she was far from London.

"Mate, we know your feelings," said Russell. "And believe it or not, we expected this reaction. We all felt the same when we first arrived. I wanted to take every little barefoot boy to a soccer game. It couldn't be done, but I could buy some soccer balls and get up a game with them. Now you see soccer balls being kicked all over the barrio.

"We can't do everything but we can do *some* things, and that does not mean that we cannot have a sanctuary for our worship."

Paul was baffled at where these comments were leading until finally Nigel spoke again. "I think we all agree completely to keep a presence in the barrio. Have you ever noticed how men and women continually walk past and slow down almost reverently? Your presence and the presence of a holy space is meaningful even if they never enter into the mission. They love to see you in your collar and cross.

"Paul, we can do both. The storefront is little expense, and you have already settled into it comfortably. Let's keep it, and you can use as you choose. Have a weekday service and continue the Bible classes for the children and adults."

Another of the founding group added, "The money for the formal church building has already been appropriated and donated for that purpose. Some of the donors are no longer living, and the church will be their legacy.

"We need the church built so that we can be fed at the altar on Sunday and continue teaching soccer, distributing bags of rice, mosquito nets and maybe even introduce a birth control study.

"But we need the church. We need this bit of home on a Sabbath, but the Filipinos also need it. It is a tribute to them to have a hallowed and lasting church in their midst. It means we are a part of them, and we are here to stay. Some will attend but not all, but it will still be their church."

Another American spoke. "Don't worry. We won't pull them inside and give them a dose of western Christianity."

A big Irishman named Colin offered thoughts Paul had not considered. "Have you not noticed how far the Filipinos walk each day? The church won't be in the barrio, but there will be a steady trek passing it every day."

Paul paused and thankfully looked around the room. "You're right. You are all so right. We can offer them a place of friendship and acceptance. Curiosity is the beginning of change. Real change grows horizontally.

"Laura often tells me that some things should have been learned in Education 101. Well, this I learned in the first week of seminary. Thank you for opening my cloudy eyes."

"Now don't get your hopes up, Padre Barrio," said Colin. "We won't be erecting St. Patrick's Cathedral. This church will be like one you have never seen!"

It was settled, and Paul was content with the future direction. He had misjudged his body of ex-pats. As the group was leaving, Paul patted Nigel on the shoulder. "How about I get up a team and challenge your soccer team to a game. With all my children, I have done a lot of soccer coaching in my time."

Chapter VI

2000

The conventional Anglican Church vs. barrio storefront tug-of-war ended with both sides winning. Paul fully embraced planning for construction of the sanctuary.

An acre lot was cleared of rainforest growth and left only palms surrounding the area that was designated for the church and a small attached social hall. Many classes and activities would be held outside under a covered pavilion.

The storefront in the barrio would continue to serve as a chapel and offer assistance in areas of need.

Two qualified professionals who had been employed by the closed paper mill were capable and eager to design the buildings and oversee the construction. Many of the barrio men had experience with using concrete blocks, installing tile floors, and putting on roofs and were thankful to be employed. For electrical work and plumbing, workers were contracted from Manila.

An outdoor Easter service with Eucharist was held in the shadow of the half-completed structures. It was a glorious day, attended by interested Anglicans who lived in fringe areas that required a journey of several hours, every member of the founding committee, and more Filipinos than had ever attended the storefront church.

There was no precedent for "new Easter outfits" as in the States. Some feet were bare and hats seemed to be the special addition for Easter service, but they were utilized as shade from the hot sun. Children jabbered and squealed throughout the service—which somehow seemed appropriate.

At the close of the service, a couple who had been standing in the back fringe of the gathering pushed forward a small boy in a makeshift cart. The crowd parted to give them an open path to Paul. Celebratory talking and laughing gave way to silence.

Paul put out his arms as they got near. He did not know what they expected or what his response should be other than "Welcome. Peace be with you."

The father only spoke Visayan, but a young boy stepped forward to translate. "Padre Barrio, the father and the mother asks that you heal their son. He was born with no sense and cannot walk or talk. They live in the barrio and see how you love us."

With pleading eyes, the mother folded her hands as if praying and uttered words that could only be "Please, please." The gathering remained silent.

Paul was overcome with the request. He reached down, picked up the frail little body, kissed him on the forehead and knew exactly where to turn. Miraculously, a bottle of holy oil was passed to Paul by someone he did not recognize.

Paul looked at the helpful young boy. "What is his name?"

The boy turned to the child's mother. As was the Filipino custom, she gave several names derived from local languages. The assisting boy looked perplexed, but eventually came out with "Bennie." It was not part of the name given by the mother, but the helper had offered the name because he knew it would be easier for Paul to say.

To regain the attention of the gathering, Paul said, "The Lord be with you," and the gathering responded, "And also with you." Paul placed his hands on the child's head and continued with the words he knew so well.

Bennie, I lay my hands upon you in the name of our Lord and Savior Jesus Christ. Beseeching Him to uphold you and fill you with his grace, that you may know the healing power of his love. Amen.

Paul dipped his thumb into the holy oil and made the sign of the cross on Bennie's forehead, and said, *I anoint you with oil in the name of the Father, and of the Son, and of the Holy Spirit. Amen.*

He then held Bennie high above him, and said, "I present to you Bennie, a child of God."

The little boy was full of giggles when Paul placed him on the shoulder of the helper, who turned and galloped through the crowd with him. Everyone reached out to touch the little handicapped boy. After the parade of Bennie and his new friend had weaved through the entire gathering, Paul concluded the service with, "Let us bless the Lord."

"Thanks be to God" rang out loudly throughout the flock.

Paul and most of the gathering knew that Bennie was unlikely to be healed of his infirmities, but his life would change. Surely, the Holy Spirit was in that place on that Easter Sunday.

Before bidding farewell to Bennie, Laura approached the parents and offered to work with him and teach him skills that could give him a more comfortable and fuller life. The boy explained Laura's proposal to the parents and answered their questions before turning to Laura to confirm. "They will bring him to the chapel for your help each day except the Sabbath."

"O Mum, Salamat, Salamat, Salamat" was repeated many times by the overjoyed parents.

The young helper was filled with spirit from his part in the unorthodox service. He waited until the crowd was leaving before approaching Paul to say, "Padre Barrio, I have followed behind you since you have been in my land. Can I help you and learn about Jesus?"

Again, Paul was overwhelmed. Happy tears filled his eyes. "You will be my disciple to help me and help me learn to help others. What is your name?"

With a grin he answered, "Marceline Petra Hermanos," but call me Petra."

"No," said Paul. "I shall call you Peter the Rock, and on this rock, I will build my church." He knew the young man did not comprehend the meaning, but he would learn. There were many miracles ahead. There might be no healing but wellness would come.

Paul never learned who had handed him the bottle of holy oil. He only had a brief glimpse of the giver and never saw him again. From that day forward, throughout the barrio, the child would be known by all as "Bennie, the blessed."

Chapter VII

2000

Paul did not relax at home after the busy Easter season as he had customarily done on Staten Island. A typhoon could not have kept him from the storefront chapel—there was too much to do. He was as filled with joy as he had been to receive his acceptance letter from seminary.

On Easter Monday, Laura rode to the barrio with him hoping the boy and his parents would be waiting at the door. They were. Bennie was sitting in his cart with his mother beside him.

She was surprised to see her Aussie neighbor, Rhonda, chatting in barrio Visayan. Rhonda seldom came to the barrio and depended on her maids for all her shopping. She was always nicely dressed—usually in all white—and very social. Good natured kidding from locals suggested she was afraid to get in the dust of the barrio. Laura had found her to be a compatible friend.

"Well, hello to y'all," said Laura. She had continued to use her Southern "y'all," as it always brought a laugh. "Rhonda, can I help you with something before Bennie and I get started?"

"No. I'm actually here to join you and Bennie. I don't know how much experience you have with children with his condition, but I believe I might be of service."

She wondered what her friend had in mind, but was thankful for any help. She had slept little the night before as she feared that she had made an offer that she could not fulfill. "I'm willing, but I don't know if I am able. Thank you."

Rhonda explained. "For twenty years while we were still in Australia, I worked as a physical therapist. Australia is very advanced in the field. We can do this together. His condition is likely cerebral palsy, which is caused by damage to the brain during birth. He needs relief from stiffness and pain in his paralyzed limbs. I hope I can help with massages, warm baths, and exercises. You can add daily living skills and maybe even communication."

Laura knew an angel had dropped from heaven by way of Australia. "With your direction, I believe we can give this child a better life. I will do whatever it takes."

Rhonda explained their plans to the mother, who smiled a toothless smile and nodded her head vigorously.

Laura noticed that Peter had joined them when they walked inside the chapel. When Rhonda explained her plan to take Bennie to her home two days a week to soak in her whirlpool bath and give him massages and exercises, Laura questioned their ability to lift the child given that both of them were slight of stature. Peter interrupted. "I will be the one."

And so, the routine began with Laura spending three days training Bennie in the most basic life skills, and the other two days, Rhonda and Peter took Bennie to Rhonda's home for physical therapy. Both knew this would be a long-term relationship.

Communication seemed the most pressing need—Bennie was trapped and unable to express his needs. Laura had learned about augmentative communication using language boards.

Among Paul's many skills was a good hand at drawing. On small index cards, he drew simple outlines of a cup, a banana, and a large jar used as indoor plumbing in the barrio.

With the cards, Bennie could quickly let it be known when he was hungry, thirsty or needed toileting. This was a big step. Seeing how quickly he grasped the three symbols, Laura doubted that he "had no sense" as his mother expressed.

New words were added each week. Peter punched holes in the cards, covered them with clear contact sheets, and attached them to a round key ring. Soon Bennie was communicating by flipping through the cards to find the one he needed. As Peter expressed, "Da boy got plenty da sense."

News traveled fast in the barrio, and at the end of the first week, a mother with an eight-year-old Down's syndrome daughter appeared at the mission. Within the month, the group had increased to seven—including an adult woman who had lost the ability to speak from a stroke and wanted to learn use of the language board.

Before Laura and Rhonda became overwhelmed they acquired a staff of three volunteers from the ex-pat wives and a nun who was a nurse in the small Catholic clinic. Diagnosis of the conditions of all could not be determined, but the objective was to determine what was most vital for each to learn and work on that skill with a practical approach.

Peter was indispensable. He became adept at physical therapy and took every opportunity to learn from Rhonda. He also devoured her extensive library of books on the various conditions. He was able to spend all morning with the group and all afternoon and evening following Paul's every step. He was learning so fast that he was able to relieve Paul of many of his more menial duties.

Every evening, the couple shared the events of their day just as they had done in the past. A few weeks after the changes that had followed Easter, they were relaxing and sharing a rum and calimesa (a small lime similar to the Key lime) punch on the screened porch.

Paul pulled Laura close. "When I see you with the little special needs group, I know why we were brought to this place, and I am so thankful. I cannot describe my joy."

"When we first arrived," said Laura, "I knew you would find your calling, but frankly, I worried about myself. I was shocked when I first reached out to Bennie's mother. I had never planned such, but I knew that I had found my mission also. It's strange that with all my training, I took on a goal where I was completely inexperienced—at a loss for how to proceed."

Paul smiled. "I had no fear of it not succeeding. When you combine a Columbia University Ph.D., a board-certified Australian physical therapist, and a young man filled with compassion and abounding love, how can that not be divine?"

Once the new sanctuary was completed, the congregation seemed to increase each Sunday. The ex-pats from the fringe areas attended regularly. Paul now understood what his early founders had meant about the conventional Anglican service being needed by folks far from home. Things were happening in the barrio *and* in the formal sanctuary. There was a need for both.

The crushing desire that Paul had in the beginning—to put most of his effort into trying to meet the basic needs of the people—was better accomplished now that he worked through agencies, foundations and the National Church. He quickly acknowledged that with their help, more could be accomplished. They could attack issues instead of only providing temporary relief.

One easy example was providing education on the dangers of unsafe drinking water. In a sermon, he paraphrased a quote everyone understood and explained, "If we give everyone in the rainforest a bottle of clean water, tomorrow we will have to give them another. If we go out and teach them to drink from running springs—which abound near them—instead of from the polluted rivers, we will not need to return."

This truth became even more forceful when a grant was funded and cases of insect-treated mosquito nets arrived for distribution in the barrio and rainforest.

When asked if he planned to cover all of Mindanao with mosquito nets, Paul had a ready reply. "No, but that does not stop us from covering everyone we can."

This relieved a sadness among all the ex-pats who had felt inadequate in face of enormous challenges. A member of the group of ex-pats felt encouraged and shared his feelings with Paul. "When parents get up in the morning and see dead mosquitoes outside of the nets, they have proof their children are being protected. What peace this must give."

Days were filled and rich with satisfaction for Laura as well as Paul. The "least of these" had always been her first priority, and the little group that began with Bennie continued to grow and thrive. As the number of participants grew, the number of volunteers kept pace. After many suggestions, the group was given the name "Children of God," but to the population of the barrio it was known as "Mam Padre Barrio." Wellness can come without healing.

From the whirlpool baths and the soothing hands of Rhonda and Peter, Bennie's lower limbs became flexible and dangled comfortably. He gained independence with the use of his communication cards and was always happy and affectionate. He became their poster child, encouraging child after child and even some adults.

Letters and pictures from family and friends kept Paul and Laura's home ties close. They were allowed a six-week sabbatical each year to return home. Thoughts of this soothed the pangs of homesickness. To celebrate Christmas season with their children and grandchildren was tempting, but how could they bear leaving their church during this of all seasons? Throughout the barrio, and with the ex-pats, Christmas was in the air long before December. Paul began to realize that all the people in this little-known part of the world waited the whole year for the birth of the Christ Child. To them it was personal and intimate.

The celebration started with Advent and continued until the end of Epiphany. Every sacred part of the story was cherished and glorified with music, tableaus, enactments and services. There would be no elaborate decorations and lights, no stores running over with toys. There would be no Santa on every corner as with most American or western Christmases. The Filipinos would celebrate the nativity as if they were family—which is how they felt as children of God.

When Paul made the first announcement for Advent celebrations, there was no doubt that the church and chapel were preparing for a celebration native-style.

 Peter had worried that his beloved hero would miss this celebration of Christmas. When Paul announced that he and Laura would be celebrating their first Filipino noel, the boy was overjoyed and bragged to them, "We will have oranges, oranges from Israel."

Oranges were only found in the barrio markets during the Christmas season and considered sacred fruit. To ensure that oranges from Israel could be given to all, Paul arranged with a merchant in the barrio to order extra crates of these precious fruits from the Holy Land.

Laura became more comfortable with the thought of Christmas without her children and grandchildren when their youngest daughter, Marie, wrote that she was making reservations to spend her two-week holiday from grad school classes to share their Filipino Christmas.

Paul did not plan events except for the Christmas Eve and Christmas Day services. Traditional observances came from the hearts of the people. He did not know what to expect until it happened.

Marie arrived in Davao on the small plane from Manila on December 23. Her parents met her and drove the route around the rainforest to reach their new home. She was astonished that her parents really lived so near the jungle.

Because of the season, the narrow road was filled with walkers. Her father had made sure to bring a supply of candy and oranges to pass out to them.

This was a new world that this New York daughter could never have imagined. On Christmas Eve before leaving for the first midnight mass at Holy Nativity, Marie called out, "Mom, Dad, come look. What is happening?"

They rushed to the door and witnessed a tradition that even Paul had never known. A procession was heading to homes on the hill, led by a young man leading a small burro with a young woman sitting atop. A crowd followed singing noels in Visayan. They all watched as the couple and burro stopped at each house and the man knocked on the door. The doors were opened and then closed quickly. When the procession reached their home, Paul knew exactly what was happening.

Paul opened the door with Laura and Marie looking over his shoulder. "Katulog na (to sleep)" the young man asked.

Curtly, Paul answered, "No room," and closed the door. He turned to face his family with a look of intense pain, "Do you realize what I just did?"

This expressed the feeling of desperation and hopelessness that the expectant father, Joseph, would have felt. The candle light mass was glorious with musicians from the barrio playing the carols that all loved. "Maayong Pastro" (Good Christmas) filled the air as most made a candle-lit walk to their homes.

For the rest of her visit, Marie spent the mornings with her mother and the children. She was a capable assistant and gave helpful suggestions. Her heart was touched by the great need and limited resources. She returned home an advocate for the handicapped in remote areas. She made contacts that made the way easier for her parents to reach the right sources for assistance.

Chapter VIII
2001-2005

After Epiphany had come and gone, Paul made detailed plans to keep the church and mission functional during the six-week respite he and Laura would take. The litanies, lessons and short message would be given by layman, including Peter, and Bible studies in the mission would continue as usual. Eucharist would be given twice by Canon Juan Tomas from the Cathedral in Davao. Rhonda, Peter and other volunteers would continue serving the special-needs children. In one year, they had established a church family strong enough for the priest to leave, secure that the church would continue as always.

Both needed the time to reunite with their family and tell their experiences to institutions, sponsors and friends who had sent support when asked. It was also a time to reflect and evaluate the effectiveness of their service.

The time passed quickly and their plans were achieved. Saying a long goodbye to their family was difficult, but they were eager to return to Mindanao. The long flight over the ocean gave Paul and Laura an uninterrupted period to talk over something that was troubling both. They had made references to the situation before, but had never had a full discussion.

"How well do you really know Peter?" asked Laura.

Paul shrugged. "I know his heart. I know his dedication. I know his mother brought him into the barrio from the rainforest to go to school when she knew that her death was near. Beyond that, I know that he is brilliant in many ways and would take advantage of more education."

"Does he have a permanent place to live? How does he support himself?"

"He usually sleeps in back of the apothecary shop. Mrs. Nunez lets him do this in exchange for his guarding the shop in the evening. Seems she has items attractive for thieves. He seems to get his food easily from wherever he happens to be at mealtime. The barrio folks are always generous."

"And," he said sheepishly, "I've been paying him a small stipend from our own purse."

Laura laughed out loud. "Well, he's double dipping. I've been giving him a small amount, too, along with the many dinners he eats with us."

Paul didn't tell her that he had already known about Laura's gifts because Peter had asked him if it was appropriate. "Whatever he receives is well deserved. I have a feeling he is saving in hope of someday finding a place for more education."

"Let's adopt him! He's not yet of legal age." Laura surprised even herself as the words came out.

"Adopt him! How many children do we need?"

"We don't need any more but he needs a family. If we adopt him, we can send him away to school. I have been reading about the Bishop Brent International School in Baguio. We can easily afford to send him there, and he would learn better English. All the subjects that are part of formal education are available. And seminary just might be in his future."

"Babe, you're putting the cart way before the horse…which I have seen you do before. First, let's investigate more. Adoption might be prohibited, and he might not want to be adopted or go to school on Luzon."

Laura sat back in her seat. "You're right. We do need more information, but oh, how I would love to see him rise up and be a leader for his countrymen."

That ended the discussion of Peter's future, but it would remain on their minds and in their hearts.

When they returned to the church and mission they found that not only was everything in good order, but attendance at Sunday service and chapel activities had been strong in their absence. From reports given by Peter and lay ministers, Paul was delighted to know that other than the blessings which only could be administered by an ordained priest, the parish could stand on its own.

That had been his purpose when given the assignment, but it did not mean he was thinking of leaving. He still had many plans, and he dearly loved being on this remote assignment. Originally, his tenue was one year, but that was never considered after the first year ended.

Peter's birthday was celebrated before the beginning of Lent. He had no birth certificate but maintained that he was born on March 5 and would turn sixteen.

They took his word and planned his first birthday party. The church grounds were filled with friends from church and the barrio, and tables of food filled the pavilion. He was showered with gifts from folks who had little to give.

Special time was given for Bennie the Blessed to present his gift of a wall cross that he had molded from clay and baked. Peter was so overwhelmed that his response was to put Bennie on his shoulders and weave through the crowd in a parade as he had done on the day of Bennie's blessing.

The birthday cake was brought out, and a blending of Visayan and English with several accents joined in singing "Happy Birthday to Peter."

Paul and Laura invited Peter to spend the night at their house. They had a special gift and wanted private time with him. They had been investigating his citizenship status and the legalities of adoption. Since he had no known living relatives, the solicitor they consulted in Manila said the adoption would be legal, but that he had only one concern.

"I applaud you for the plans you have for this young man. When your time here ends, do you plan to take him to the United States?"

Paul had already given this much thought. "If he is still in school in Baggio, probably not. Later it will depend on his wishes."

The barrister thought for a few moments before expressing his feelings. "I must be honest with you. I appreciate your affection for this young man, and I know you could give him a secure future and opportunities in America. He is bright. He will take advantage of an education and would be an asset to his homeland, especially when he knows the life so well. I grieve to lose a young man who could make such a difference for his people on Mindanao."

Laura spoke. "Our only concern is that he has good care and will receive an education before we return home permanently."

They had sought out a counselor who was well-versed in Filipino law and how it applied to their unique situation. The alternatives he presented showed they had made a good choice.

"If you are granted a guardianship of him until he becomes of age at twenty-one, you can include the provision that you will provide for his welfare and education. I think that will allow you to do all that you desire for him while allowing him to keep his Filipino citizenship. That is not as difficult to do as obtaining permission for adoption and changing his citizenship."

This suited them perfectly except for one assurance which Paul demanded. "Can he visit the United States for extended periods of time? This is important in case he would like to come for higher education. Also, if he should choose, could he apply for U.S. citizenship?"

"Yes, yes, as long as your guardianship applies. He would have to apply the same as other Filipinos, but with your sponsorship, that should not be a problem."

On the night of his sixteenth birthday, Peter was presented with this proposal. His first answer was definite, "I want to go away for education, Padre Barrio, and I want to learn and help my people. I will always be a Filipino, but someday I want to go to Disney World."

In his research, Paul found that the Bishop Brent International School in Baggio was founded in 1909 by the first missionary bishop to the Philippines, in response to requests from American parents for a boarding school for their children. Despite the attendance of the children of expatriates, the majority of enrollees are Filipinos. Some are from well-to-do families but many are on scholarships.

They talked with many friends whose children had attended or graduated from the school. Everyone gave an excellent recommendation. Paul made up his mind after talking with the bishop in Davao. His son had recently graduated from the secondary school and was now in university in Australia.

Laura, Paul and Peter made a visit to the school and were especially impressed that students were able to move through the courses at their own pace. Since Peter had no records of achievement in secondary school, this arrangement suited his needs. He would be tested in each required course and placed at his achievement level.

The professors were impressed with the maturity and composure of this boy from one of the most limited provinces in their country. After interviews with several priests and educators, Peter was accepted. His Padre Barrio and Mam Padre Barrio had never been any prouder. Their attachment to him was strong, and although he would be hundreds of miles away, this was his chance in life.

He qualified for scholarships, but his family declined. They could easily pay his expenses and felt the scholarships should be reserved for others with the need of financial help.

Baggio is in the north of Luzon, a mountainous region and the summer capital of the Philippines. The government summers there to escape the oppressive heat of Manila.

They definitely would enjoy visiting their boy. It would be a long journey but also a place to refresh and relax from their arduous life. "Iceberg lettuce grows there," said Laura. "Of everything, I have missed salads most of all."

A month later Peter boarded a plane to Manila where he would change to a flight to Baggio. His uniforms and other essentials had been ordered and would be awaiting him. Laura was tempted to escort him, but Paul said a definitive "No." They waved goodbye at the Davao airport and returned home in the little Datsun to an empty nest.

The next two years passed quickly. Peter returned home on breaks from classes and a long break at Christmas and Easter. He was no longer a boy. He spoke, looked and behaved with maturity. The barrio regarded him as their hero, and he was always followed by a trail of children.

At the end of his third year, Peter had completed all requirements for a diploma from secondary school. He was nineteen. University was the next step.

He joined Laura and Paul on a trip to United States and loved seeing the country that was admired all over the world. A quick trip to Disney World overwhelmed him.

Paul arranged visits for him with several colleges in New England and New York. Laura demanded equal time for the South, and they toured Emory and Duke. He handled the visits well and could have been accepted at each, but he was set and determined that he wanted an education in his homeland. His dream and goal was to be a part of the betterment of the lives of his fellow Filipinos. Both foster parents lauded him for this.

His choice of a place of higher learning was The University of the Philippines in Manila. He had studied the catalogues and wanted to study social science, which would open many opportunities for service.

Secretly, he still nursed the vow he had made to Paul on the day of Bennie's blessing. "I want to help you, Padre Barrio, and learn about Jesus."

Life in Manila was far more hectic than Baggio and more complicated than Mindanao, but Peter learned valuable skills. He quickly adjusted to the noise and commotion of the crowds and jeepneys filled with passengers darting through the streets at peril to pedestrians. "Jeepneys" were vehicles made from U.S. military jeeps left behind after WWII, known for their flamboyant decorations and crowded seating.

Time had flown. Although they'd originally committed to one year of service, Paul and Laura had completed their fifth year of the mission assignment. During those five years, the countenance of the parish—and even the barrio—had changed. The storefront mission had doubled in size and now occupied an adjacent storefront. This allowed for space for the school for special needs and small classrooms for volunteers who were offering training in practical areas. A little used clubhouse, remnant of the defunct paper mill, was outfitted by ex-pats with a whirlpool, a sauna, and exercise equipment. The ex-pats soon found it to be an aid to them as well as the special needs children.

When Rhonda and her husband decided to return to Australia, they outfitted their van with a lift, and donated it to the school. This transportation gave more opportunity for therapy. The year prior to their leaving, Rhonda trained a young Filipino woman to replace her. She was very adept and followed all of Rhonda's procedures. The therapy was left in good hands.

None of the services could have existed without the volunteers. Almost every ex-pat had a special skill which could be taught and added as a skill to a Filipino. Their lifestyles improved when they were useful again.

Ladies who had spent their mornings leisurely at home with helpers taking care of all needs and their afternoon sitting around a pool gossiping and enjoying a too early cocktail time, were now working daily at the church, mission or in the school.

Paul now understood what his mentor meant when he told him on the day he proposed the mission, "These people are far from home and need an established church for worship." Life had been enriched for the ex-pats along with the residents of the barrio.

Chapter IX
2006

As they entered year six of their mission, both Paul and Laura were over seventy. Health became a concern. Arthritis was beginning to take a toll on Paul, and Laura seemed to have some of the ailments that she remembered from her grandmother, Myra. She always had latent fear when she thought of the early deaths of her mother and father from cardiovascular issues.

Neither shared their concerns with the other, but both knew that age and their heavy responsibilities would make it unwise for them to continue living in such a remote place with limited medical care.

Peter completed his studies at University of the Philippines with high honors and would graduate in June. He had kept his future plans to himself, and they wanted him to be free to make his decision without interference from their opinions. They had consoled themselves long before that Peter would always be a part of their life, but they knew his heart would always be on Mindanao.

They made appointments to check into a diagnostic clinic in Manila during the week of his graduation and have thorough physicals. The two days at the clinic would be their secret. Then they would move into a hotel and enjoy the festivities of their boy receiving his university degree.

On a static-filled telephone call, Peter told them of his excitement of seeing them and joining their annual trip to the United States. He also announced that he had a surprise.

"Would this surprise deal with a girl?" Paul asked. This was a question often asked. They wanted him to have family, especially when the time came for them to return permanently to the United States.

At the clinic they shared a room, but went their separate ways for the examinations. Neither discussed the procedures until the last evening. They checked into the hotel and went to the dining room for a quiet dinner. Peter did not plan to see them until the next day.

The hotel and dining room meal was a luxury which they enjoyed. After martinis, a steak, and a large crisp salad, it was time to talk.

Paul started first. "My results showed that for a man my age I am in good shape. The arthritis can be helped with medication, and he also suggests a place with a cooler climate. I told him I can't change the climate of Mindanao. So how about you, Babe?"

Laura's first concern was for her husband. "Dear, you know the heat and humidity are hard on you. You can't just depend on pills. Let's give this more thought. Maybe you could find a mission in Baggio."

"Does iceberg lettuce have a bearing on this?"

"Of course, not. My only thoughts are for a way to remain in the Philippines and improve your health."

"And stay close to Peter." Paul knew that had a bearing for both he and Laura.

When they began to feel comfortable with the conversation, there was more to share. "I know you have always been concerned about your heart, blood pressure and kidney function since those conditions have been in your family," said Paul. "Do you have reports on this?"

"Yes, and all are normal…but…there is something else."

Paul stopped short. "So, tell me, darling."

"I am sure this is minor, but the gynecologist thought it should be checked further."

"Gynecologist? You're not pregnant, are you?" Both of them broke into laughter. Finally, Laura became serious again.

"No, but he did find a suspicious lesion in my right breast that needs further attention. I can do that while we are home."

Paul stared at the candles. "I have to be honest. I fudged a bit on my report. The doctor thinks this could turn into a crippling condition. I have no interest in going to Baggio or any other place in the Philippines except our little haven on Mindanao and that is where I cannot stay." He took a deep breath. "And you, my bride, must go to Columbia Medical and have the finest treatment the U.S. has to offer."

Laura nodded. "Yes, Paul, it is time to go home. We will tell Peter after he shares his surprise."

Plans were for Peter to meet them the next morning for breakfast in the hotel dining room. During the evening, they discussed the words to use when giving him the news without alarming him unnecessarily.

Paul was also concerned that his ward would feel they were deserting the church or the people. "I want him to know that I am leaving a church that is strongly established and will continue to thrive with a new and younger priest."

"Who will that be? I can't believe they will be without an ordained priest for a long period of time." Laura did not know that this had been discussed by Paul and the bishop of Davao on many occasions. Both wanted to have plans in place for the inevitable time of Paul returning to his homeland.

"It will be quite tempting for a priest to come to a place with a thriving parish, a sanctuary awaiting, and to live in this amazing place. There are several young Filipino deacons now stationed at the cathedral and awaiting ordination. Bishop thinks highly of each, and joins me in feeling it is time for a Filipino priest to lead the people."

The next morning, they sat in the dining room, sipping coffee and eager to see their grown up, handsome son. "There he is—and look—he does have a surprise! A girl is with him." Laura could not resist racing to meet him at the door, and Paul was right behind.

After warm embraces and kisses, Peter took the young lady's hand and brought her forward. They were surprised to see that she was not Filipino. She was a lovely blue-eyed blond with a complexion that told them she was British.

During his years away in schools, he had stopped referring to his Padre Barrio and Mam Padre Barrio. "Mom, Dad, this is my girlfriend, Diana Radcliffe. We have been dating during the past year at university. She will be receiving her degree tomorrow also."

"I am honored to finally meet Pete's parents. I admire your work on Mindanao and know the value." As soon as she spoke there was no doubt that she was British.

They were almost at a loss for words but exchanged all the pleasantries of introductions. Conversation at the table tried to cover all their time apart quickly and get to know this young lady who had been an unknown part of their son's life.

They learned that her family was from London but she had been brought up in Hong Kong where her father managed a British bank. Her schooling had been in Switzerland and England until college when she chose the University of the Philippines to be more diversified after participating in a student exchange program for a summer semester.

They overate from the breakfast buffet, which included both western and eastern dishes. Conversation turned to plans for the graduation the next day until Peter interrupted. "I think it is time that I show you my surprise. Are you ready?"

"Yes, yes we are eager to hear." Laura had thought the unexpected girlfriend had been the surprise, and she was quite happy and content with that.

Peter handed Paul an open envelope. Paul glanced at the return address, written in Tagalog, the language of Luzon. It was easy to identify as Saint Andrews Theological Seminary. He studied the letter carefully before breaking into a broad smile and grabbing the boy's hand.

"What is it? Tell me!"

Paul handed the letter to her to read. She burst into tears of joy. "Our son has been accepted to seminary. We are the parents of a future priest. Praise God from whom all blessings flow."

Paul had attended a service at Saint Andrews once when he was in Manila. "Isn't that the chapel with the boat hanging from the ceiling?"

"Yes, I love it. 'I will make you fishers of men.' That is why I so wanted to receive my holy orders from Saint Andrews. It reminds me of home."

After discussing all the details and future aspirations, Peter wanted to tell Diana's plans also. "She has been accepted into Medical School at University of the Philippines. We will both be here in Manila for the next four years. After that will be internships—maybe in the states. After I am ordained and Diana finishes her residency, we will return to Mindanao for our careers. I will always serve my island."

"Wow! Those plans cover everything. I know you will accomplish every step. I cannot tell you how proud I am that you will return to Mindanao. What a team you will make." Laura took note that marriage had not been mentioned, but time would tell.

Paul thought back to the day they met. "By that time Bennie the Blessed will be a grown man. You must find a place for him on your staff. Remember, he started all of this for you."

"I do remember," said Peter. "I told you I wanted to learn about Jesus, and I did. Sometimes I think I do not need seminary, for I have learned from you."

The morning ended with the disclosure of Paul and Laura's medical issues and the need to permanently return to the United States. Peter's reaction was better than expected. He wanted them to take care of their health and knew this could be better done by specialists in the States. He did have one request—an airplane ticket at least once a year.

Paul winked at Diana. "How about two tickets…twice a year?"

Chapter X
2007

Because of the medical issues, both Paul and Laura needed to return to the states without delay. All preparations were made in three weeks time for them to leave their home, friends and beloved parish. The bishop chose a young Filipino priest on his staff that he immediately assigned as a priest-in-charge. He would serve for a year and the parish could then call him for Holy Nativity or select another priest.

The young priest and his wife and small daughter immediately came to Baslig and moved in with Laura and Paul. This gave adequate time for the new priest to be introduced to the parish and the barrio. The young priest was ecstatic to have the opportunity to follow the famed Padre Barrio who had brought so many blessings to the area and people.

Huge wooden crates were filled with personal items to send via ship to U.S. All items Paul had presented to the church and mission would remain. Laura put most of her clothes in the clothing closet of the storefront. Inez and Lupe agreed to remain as helpers in the home. Files were saved and their computers were wiped clean and left along with printers to be used in the computer skills class of the mission. This had been a big hit with teenagers.

Two suitcases were packed with cherished souvenirs of their stay. A carry-on bag for Laura and a backpack for Paul were filled with essentials. It seemed much easier to pack than they had anticipated. One last detail remained unsolved—Lizzie, the cat. Laura had hoped the new family and especially the little girl would fall in love with her just as Laura had on arrival. Sadly, the little girl was afraid of gentle Lizzie, and the mother did not want an animal in the house.

Laura would have loved taking Lizzie to the United States. That was not only impossible but unwise since she would have to be crated and sent with baggage.

This heartbreak was prevented when Peter arrived to assist in the move. Lizzie adored him and was in his lap or following in his footsteps every moment. After Laura explained her despair, he immediately said, "She's my cat also. I will have an apartment so all I need is a litter box. Diana and I will take her and care for her."

After that, Laura felt more at ease with the move. She began to notice that Diana was included in all of Peter's plans. Time will tell, she thought. Peter stayed to help with the packing and would return to Manila with them. On the small plane flight to Manila, carrying a cat on board would be nothing unusual—they remembered their first flight to Mindanao and the surprise of seeing chickens, pigs and even a goat.

Much of the remaining time was taken up with farewell parties from their friends and the church. There was even a parade and street dance in the barrio. The main attraction was Peter weaving through the parade with Bennie on his back just as on the day when the boy was blessed—not healed but made whole. Many thanks were given and many tears were shed. Peter recorded it all with a movie camera and promised a copy would be sent to the mission.

On the day of departure, when the little Datsun headed up the road to catch the plane in Davao, the roads were lined with throngs of people waving goodbye. The car would be left with the bishop awaiting the need of a future priest. Paul, Laura, and Peter needed to make this drive together and alone.

When the car reached the edge of the rainforest, people came out of the jungle to wave goodbye. Love poured out for Padre Barrio and the Mam.

Diana met them, and she and Peter waited the several hours until they boarded the plane for San Francisco. It was difficult to say goodbye to their beloved boy, but they felt secure in his future happiness and service. They would return for his graduation and ordination.

After his acceptance to seminary, Peter had decided to postpone his visit to U.S. and spend the few weeks getting prepared to begin his seminary studies. The decision was also influenced by his insight that his Mom and Dad preferred to be alone as their medical issues were addressed. Also, their five other children would be near if needed.

As the plane left the mainland, Laura stared out the window watching the island of Luzon disappear. She thought of the time after she had said her last goodbye to her grandmother,

Myra, and she watched out the plane window as her home state of Georgia disappeared. It was a feeling she knew well.

"Paul, will you get my carry-on?"

He didn't ask why but reached up and handed it down to her. She unzipped it and pulled out a bulky, well-worn red book. Embossed on the front were these words:

New Revised Standard Bible
Large Print Edition
Myra Stuart MacTavish

Laura held it close to her heart.

She had been just a little girl when her family had gathered under the pecan trees in Uncle Stephen's yard, and Grandma Myra had been presented the Bible in celebration of her learning to read.

At first, her grandmother had protested that she could not read the strange words. The children insisted that she could read this Bible. She opened and stared at the first words of Genesis and began to read, "In the beginning God created the heaven and the earth."

She could read every word, and for the rest of her life the red Bible was close by at all times. As Laura was saying goodbye and preparing to leave after her grandmother's funeral, Uncle Stephen had handed her a paper bag. "Mama would want you to have this. Take care of it and read it."

She flipped through the pages and found that each page had verses underlined with a blunt point pencil. Sometime a comment was scribbled in the margin. A red ribbon marker opened to the book of Matthew. Underlined heavily with the pencil were these words:

> *Truly I tell you, just as you did it unto*
> *the least of these, you did it unto me.*
> *(Matthew 25:40)*

Laura closed her eyes and reached for Paul's hands.

Dear Grandma, most of your life you were one of the least of these, and you told me that others did unto you. This is how you lived your life. Help me to always remember. Thank you.

I love you.

Your granddaughter,

Laura Jean

Epilogue

Returning to life in the United States was an adjustment neither Paul nor Laura had considered. They were at first overwhelmed by the rapid pace and abundance of material wealth. This was their home and much family was nearby, but they never lost their longing for the serenity and simplicity of life with their Filipino friends.

Heath issues were the first concern before any future plans could be made. Laura had the needed surgery and underwent a long round of cancer treatments before being pronounced well.

For the remainder of his life, Paul's crippling arthritis could only be alleviated by medications and physical therapy. His mobility relied on an electric wheelchair. A lift-van and the chair kept him and Laura involved in church and the breakfast program in Greenwich Village. Laura quickly returned to being the "Grits Lady," and Paul was essential for carrying the grits and supplies in his lap as he buzzed into the building.

Their last visit to the Philippines was to attend the graduation of Peter, their Filipino son, from seminary, his ordination as a deacon and his wedding to Diana.

Accommodations were made for Paul to unite the couple in marriage and both Peter and Diana returned to the United States with them. He would serve as a deacon for a year at a large church on Manhattan. Diana would serve her residency at Columbia Medical.

Future plans were to return to Philippines and serve in areas of need. Their ambitions were fulfilled, and Peter was ordained as a priest by the bishop in the cathedral at Davao. Peter arranged for the complete ordination to be filmed for his parents. They would watch the film many times, always pausing at the same scene—Bennie the Blessed and his mother sitting on one of the front pews.

May the Lord of hope fill you with joy and peace in believing, so that you may abound in hope by the power of the Holy Spirit.
Romans 15:13

Acknowledgments

I thank my late husband Al and children John, Jeff and Erin for support and much material for my writing.

About the Author

After 24 years teaching special needs students, enjoying the growth of three children, and following her husband's career to different locations, retirement gave the chance to accomplish Shirley Twiss's dream of writing. She now lives in Greenville, S.C. and fills her life with family, friends, volunteering, church, some travel, writing a weekly column for her hometown paper, *The Swainsboro Forest Blade*, and…publishing books.

She describes herself as neither a writer nor storyteller but a story keeper. Her vault is still filled with stories.